# ANOTHER
# SANIBEL
# SUNSET
# DETECTIVE

## Also by Ron Base

### Fiction
*Matinee Idol*
*Foreign Object*
*Splendido*
*Magic Man*
*The Strange*
*The Sanibel Sunset Detective*
*The Sanibel Sunset Detective Returns*

### Non-fiction
*The Movies of the Eighties* (with David Haslam)
*If the Other Guy Isn't Jack Nicholson, I've Got the Part*
*Marquee Guide to Movies on Video*
*Cuba Portrait of an Island* (with Donald Nausbuam)

**www.ronbase.com**
Read Ron's blog at
**www.ronbase.wordpress.com**
Contact Ron at
**ronbase@ronbase.com**

# ANOTHER SANIBEL SUNSET DETECTIVE

a novel

# RON BASE

West-End
Books

Library and Archives Canada Cataloguing in Publication
Base, Ron, 1948-
        Another Sanibel Sunset Detective / Ron Base.
ISBN 978-0-9736955-6-4
        I. Title.
PS8553.A784A64 2012        C813'.54        C2012-906903-5


West-End Books
80 Front St. East, Suite 605
Toronto, Ontario
Canada M5E 1T4

Cover Design: Bridgit Stone-Budd
Text Design: Ric Base
Electronic formatting: Ric Base
Sanibel-Captiva map: Ann Kornuta

Second Edition

For Ray Bennett
*Raymundo!*

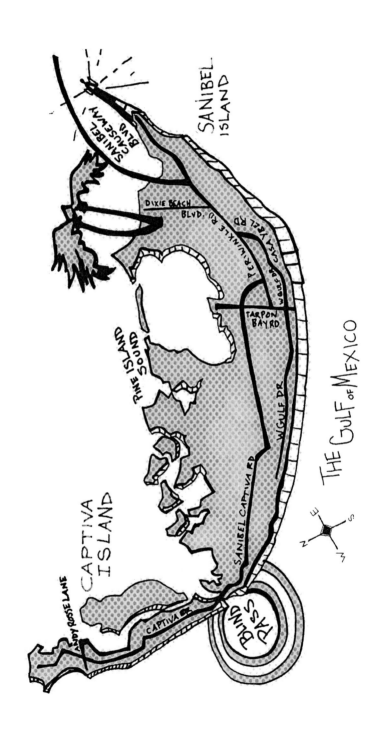

# 1

It was the night of Freddie's sixtieth birthday, and they were celebrating at Tour d'Argent, the most famous restaurant in Paris. They sat near the big windows that gave out onto a sixth floor view of Notre Dame at dusk, dramatically cast against a deepening sky that lit the barges on the Seine in a crimson glow. The comfortable purr of people with money murmuring over good food and fine wine filled the perfumed air.

You could learn to live like this, Tree Callister thought. You could forget all the things that you came to Paris to forget.

Out loud Tree said, "Francis Macomber has everything, including money and a beautiful wife. Why he probably ate regularly at this very restaurant."

"He could be here tonight," Freddie Stayner said.

"Francis is on safari in Africa, hunting lions, anxious to test himself, the limits of his courage. But when he is finally confronted with a lion, when it gets right down to it, he turns and runs. Francis is a coward."

"You know you tell me the story of Francis Macomber every time we come to Paris," Freddie said.

"That's because of all the things Hemingway wrote, including *The Sun Also Rises*, his masterpiece—the novel that caused me to fall in love with Paris—I keep coming back to *The Short Happy Life of Francis Macomber*."

"You and Hemingway and Paris," Freddie said. "What is it about the three of you?"

"I'm not quite sure," Tree said. "I think it started when I was a rookie reporter, that's when I read Hemingway's Francis Macomber story. It haunted me."

"I think it still haunts you," Freddie said.

"Maybe you're right. I keep wondering what would happen if I was in Macomber's shoes. Would I run from the lion?"

"If you were smart, you would," Freddie said.

"Anyway, from my vantage point in Chicago, Hemingway and Paris looked like the last word in hard-boiled romanticism. In those days, we were all trying to imitate Hemingway, or what we naively thought was supposed to be Hemingway."

"Hemingway killed himself," Freddie said.

"A few of us even tried to duplicate that part," Tree said.

The waiter appeared and Freddie insisted they begin with quenelles de brochet, pike dumplings.

"The dumplings are made with fish," Freddie explained when the food arrived. "They originated in Lyon where there are lots of pike."

"They're delicious," Tree said, digging his fork into the soft flesh of a dumpling.

"Particularly with the Nantua sauce."

"The what?"

"The creamy sauce that comes with it. I think they used crayfish tonight, although you can use lobster."

"Is there anything you don't know?" Tree said.

"Too many things," Freddie answered. "For instance, I don't know what the future holds. I wish I did. It would make things so much easier."

"We are not in Paris for the future," Tree said, hoping to deflect Freddie from pursuing this line. "Maybe the past, a little bit. But otherwise we live in the moment, and we don't worry about anything else."

"Wouldn't you?" Freddie persisted. "Wouldn't you like to know what happens?"

"I know what happens. We die. That's what happens. What's worse, we are closer to the end of it all then we are to the beginning. We know what's going to happen, and every day we get closer to it—except in Paris. Here, you get the impression you could live forever. At least, I do."

She gazed at him for a long time before she said, "In the meantime, we have problems, Tree, and they don't seem to be going away very fast."

"I know that," he said. "But it's your birthday and Paris is our escape together, so let's concentrate on that."

"Paris doesn't seem to be working its magic this time," Freddie said.

Tree saw the unexpected tear run down her cheek. He took her hand in his. The noise of the rich eating and laughing and having the time of their lives rose up around them.

"I'm sorry," she said quietly. "I shouldn't have had that second glass of wine."

"You haven't had a second glass."

"Well, don't let me order one." She wiped the tears away. "Then I really will be out of control."

He held her hand tighter. "Let's just enjoy ourselves tonight," he said. "Tonight there is only us in Paris."

She forced a smile as she lifted her wine glass. "To Paris," Freddie said. "Where there are no problems. There is only Paris."

"More than enough for anyone," Tree said.

"At least for tonight," Freddie said.

"Happy birthday, my darling," he said.

"Yes," she said, and tried to sound happy when she said it.

They touched their glasses together, and kissed, and the servers chose that moment to arrive with their main courses: the sole farcie for him; the roti for her. They finished dinner without further discussion of problems, real or imagined. Tree asked their waiter to take a photograph, the two of them holding hands, staring wide-eyed into the camera. When he looked at the photo later, Freddie's smile appeared plastered on, as if someone had attached it to an unhappy face. Her eyes looked dead. Or was he imagining that?

They floated out of the restaurant and down the elevator onto the street where they proceeded to walk hand in hand along the Seine, Paris all around them, now cast in a deep evening blue, the light provided by passing bateaux mouche and the lamps along the quays and on the bridges.

On a night like this, your stomach full of good food, holding the hand of the woman you loved more than any other single person in the world, you were supposed to be happy, without a care in the world, feeling the lightness and joie de vivre of Gene Kelly in *An American In Paris*.

But Freddie's outburst only served to confirm the cloud that hovered over the evening, a cloud that not even walking beside the Seine could lift. Tree tried not to think about the recent traumatic upheavals in their lives on Sanibel Island, Florida, and their effect on their marriage. Seismic changes had occurred since an aging ex-newspaperman, desperate to reinvent himself, had decided to become a private detective. All that was for another time.

That's what he tried to tell himself.

When it was finally dark, they found a cab that transported them through narrow streets to the apartment they had rented for the week. It was located in a part of the city known as Montorgueil, haunt of the so-called Bobos, according to Freddie, a contraction of Bourgeois and Bohemian, the new fashionables of Paris, young people with a lot of money pretending they had no money at all. No wonder Tree felt out of place. He was a person with no money, in Paris pretending he had a lot of it.

Their apartment was off Rue Montorgueil, along a cobblestoned thoroughfare full of shops now closed for the night. They climbed the three floors to their combination sitting room and bedroom, with French windows that opened to the street. A gentle breeze stirred the curtains. Somewhere below a passerby sang at the top of his lungs.

The nameless song drifted away as Freddie and Tree made the sort of love you can only make in Paris—the kind of love that drives all the bad things away, that lodges forever in memory.

Paris love.

# 2

Late the next afternoon, after a day of sightseeing, they returned to their apartment, and Freddie finally admitted she was feeling awful. "I don't know what's wrong with me," she said.

She lay down on the bed and allowed Tree to place a blanket over her. She murmured thanks and seconds later fell into a deep sleep.

When she awoke again, it was eight o'clock. Tree got her some water. She said she was feeling better, just tired and wanting more sleep. She wasn't hungry, she said. But if he was, he should go out for something.

"I don't want to leave you." Tree said.

"Don't be ridiculous," Freddie said. "You don't have to starve yourself to death for me."

"I'll grab something fast, and come right back," Tree said.

"Take your time. All I want to do is sleep."

Was that all she wanted? Tree wondered. Maybe she also desired time alone without him. He splashed water on his face and put on a blazer. By then Freddie was sound asleep again.

Trying to shake off the unease he had been feeling practically since their plane landed, not at all helped by Freddie's abrupt exit from the evening, he walked along rue Dussoubs to rue Montorgueil. The streets were filled with young people, everyone seemingly preoccupied with their cell phones. It struck Tree that he was not young and he did not have his cell phone with him. He felt suddenly downright elderly and out of place and curiously vulnerable. Being on the town in Paris by himself lacked the appeal it once had.

He spotted that rarest of things in Paris at night—a taxi without a passenger. Suddenly, he knew where he wanted to go. When you could find no comfort in the present, the best thing was to escape to the past.

Tree jumped into the cab.

———

Curious how memory plays its tricks.

Tree remembered the bistro side of La Closerie des Lilas being much larger than the intimate dark wood ship's cabin that confronted him. It had been years since he was last here and during that time, Lilas had expanded in his mind to accommodate constantly growing memory.

A friend had brought him for lunch the first time he was in Paris in the early eighties, another of those places that had drawn Tree because it was a Hemingway hangout.

Since then, the brasserie had become something of a Paris touchstone for him although he wasn't certain why. Nothing particularly remarkable had ever happened to him here. The food was good without being memorable. Still, in the glow produced by the tiny wall lamps, with the piano player at the entrance tinkling away at Gershwin's "Summertime," Tree relaxed, feeling much more at home swimming in the nostalgia of his past than he was among the young of rue Montorgueil.

Tonight, with everyone on the terrace enjoying the summer evening, Tree pretty much had the interior of the brasserie to himself. Just him and whatever ghosts of Hemingway lingered. He occupied a stool at the end of the bar near the brass plaque marking the place Hemingway used to sit.

For a moment, Tree was tempted to order a kir royale, his drink of choice in the old days. He dismissed the impulse, asked for sparkling water and a menu. He would eat something at the bar, briefly inhale nostalgia, and then get back to poor, sick Freddie.

"Wait a minute," he said to the bartender.

"Monsieur."

"I've changed my mind. A kir royale, si'l vous plait."

Why not? he thought to himself as the bartender nodded and went away. I'm in Paris, after all, and for a single night reliving long-ago youth—a youth that would include a kir royale at La Closerie des Lilas. Or maybe two.

The bartender returned and placed a glass filled with a bright liquid the color of a pale rose on the bar in front of him. Tree stared at it for a time and then lifted the kir royale until it glittered in the light of the Closerie. He placed the edge of the glass to his lips and took a deep swallow.

The sweet, biting taste filled his mouth, and then made its way languidly through his body, as if to warm him with the memory of what it was like to sit here with a few of these inside him. Of course, it was never the first that got you into trouble. It was always the second and then the third.

Well, he thought, putting the unfinished glass back on the bar, he wasn't going to get into any trouble tonight. Those days were long over.

"You are in my seat," a voice behind him said.

He turned to find a young woman standing there. He had a sense of blonde hair tumbling around bare shoulders, a short skirt and long legs.

"Is this where you sit?" he said.

"It's where Hemingway sat, so that's where I have to sit."

Tree got off the stool to make room for her, taking his glass with him.

"You're sure you don't mind?"

"I've sat there many, many times," he said.

"I'm Cailie Fisk," she said, offering a slim hand.

He took her hand. "Tree Callister."

"Tree? That's an interesting name."

"It's short for Tremain. When I was growing up the kids all called me Tree."

"Nice to meet you, Tree."

She perched on the stool, very still, closing her eyes as though attempting to draw in the essence of Hemingway. Her eyes popped open again and she looked at him. "I wonder if he really did sit here. I mean, how does anyone really know?"

"I've thought the same thing many times."

"He does talk about the Closerie in *A Moveable Feast*, so I suppose the chances are pretty good that his elbow must have nudged this part of the bar, however inadvertently."

"I'm surprised someone your age is even interested in Hemingway."

"I'm fascinated by all things Paris," she said. "When you're growing up in St. Louis, that's a million miles from Paris, so I embraced all the clichés. The Eiffel Tower. The impressionists. Hemingway in Paris. The unrealistic, romantic view they keep for the tourists. But then I'm the kind of girl who gets to London and rushes over to see the changing of the guard at Buckingham Palace. Old things, but enduring. I like that."

The bartender came over and arched an eyebrow? "Madame?"

She ordered a kir royale.

Tree looked at her. "Why a kir royale?"

"I don't know. I read somewhere that if you came to La Closerie des Lilas you should order a kir royale. So here I am at the Closerie ordering a kir."

"That used to be my favorite drink."

"Used to be?"

"Back in my drinking days in Paris."

"What's that you're holding?"

"It's a kir royale," Tree said.

She smiled. "Your drinking days appear to have returned."

"Nostalgia overcame me for a minute there," Tree said.

"How did it taste?"

"Not quite the same."

"It never does, I guess. You came here for work?"

He said, "I was a newspaperman in Chicago."

"But you're not anymore?"

"Not for a long time."

"What do you do now?"

What to say to that? "Now I'm a private investigator on Sanibel Island in Florida."

"You're not serious."

"Some days I wonder," he said.

The bartender placed the kir royale in front of her. "What's in this?" she said.

"It's crème de cassis which is a black currant liqueur. An ordinary kir is topped with white wine. With a kir royale, they add champagne."

She lifted the glass off the bar. "To Hemingway and nights in Paris," she said.

He touched his glass to hers. "To Hemingway," he said. She took a tentative sip and smiled. "It's delicious. Are you not going to have a drink?"

"I think I've had enough," he said.

"Come on, Monsieur Tree Callister from Sanibel Island, you can't toast Hemingway and Paris and then not drink."

"Maybe you're right," he said with a grin, and finished off the rest of his kir.

His eyes watered, and he felt that warmth again. The room softened around him. Or was that his kir-fueled imagination?

"So let me see, Sanibel Island," she said. "That's off the west coast of Florida, isn't it?"

"That's right. In fact, the agency I run is called The Sanibel Sunset Detective Agency."

"And how many agents does Sanibel Sunset Detective employ?"

"Just one," Tree said.

"You?"

"I'm the Sanibel Sunset detective."

"I see. Are there many calls for private detectives on Sanibel Island?"

He laughed and shook his head. "Everyone thought I was crazy, including my wife. But there is business as it turns out."

"You're in Paris with your wife?"

"Yes, we're here celebrating her birthday." Now Tree was beginning to feel embarrassed, and the burning in his face wasn't just the result of the unexpected liquor in his system. He hastened to awkwardly explain: "She's come down with some sort of bug. I ducked out to get something to eat."

"I'm sorry to hear she's not feeling well," Cailie said. "I hope she's going to be all right."

The waiter returned and asked in English if they wanted menus. "I haven't eaten anything today and I'm starving. Have you eaten yet?"

"No, not yet," he said.

"Why not get something together, and then you can get back to your wife, and I'll go back to my lonely, miserable hotel room."

"Now I'm starting to feel sorry for you," he said.

"Maybe that's the idea."

"A beautiful young woman in Paris, you won't be lonely for long."

"In the meantime, I am hungry."

Tree thought of Freddie back at their apartment. She probably was sound asleep. And he *was* hungry, and, he had to admit, the kir royale had released something inside him. He felt loose and free tonight, like the old days in Paris. Why not dinner? He glanced around at the unoccupied tables and booths. "Why don't we sit over there against the wall?" He turned to the bartender. "Is that all right?"

"Bien sûr, monsieur."

They took their drinks to the table. Cailie sat facing him and the waiter brought the menus.

"Tell me about yourself," Tree said. "You grew up in St. Louis. Are you still there?"

She studied the menu a moment before she said, "Very much so."

"What do you do there?"

"Right now, I'm not so sure."

"No?"

"It's the sort of confusion that occurs in a life when your sister is killed, and you break off with your fiancé, and all the things you thought were certain in life suddenly aren't so certain anymore."

"I'm sorry," Tree said.

"Don't be sorry about the fiancé," she said. "He's a jerk. But my sister was a different matter. We weren't very close, but still, she was my sister. Everyone in the family was devastated, of course. My parents are having a terrible time with it. I had to get away. I've always wanted to come to Paris, and so I thought, well, if I'm ever going to do it, then maybe now is the time."

"And was that a good decision?"

She paused to consider this. "I think so," she said carefully. "Although it turns out you can't outrun your de-mons—or your memories."

"You certainly can't outrun your memories," Tree said. "That's the trouble with Paris. It holds onto them for you and waits for you to come back and then springs them on you."

"Maybe," she said with a shrug. "But I'm a newcomer, remember. So I bring dreams to Paris, not memories. Over-all, Paris has been a fine escape. I don't have to think about my sister here, I don't have to think about anything but seeing and experiencing all the things I've always dreamt about the city."

"What happened to your sister?" he asked.

Cailie appeared not to have heard the question.

A server arrived and so they ordered: the red mullet fi-let for him; simple chicken for her, accompanied by a glass of Pouilly Fuissé. He declined wine. The warming effects of the kir were beginning to wear off, leaving him with a slight buzzing in his head. He should never have had that drink. When their meals arrived, they ate pretty much in a silence filled with Gershwin and Cole Porter, and some Henry Mancini, courtesy of the piano player.

By the time they finished, the few diners inside the brasserie had departed. The piano player had closed down for the night. Tree ordered the check, feeling a lot more sober and somewhat relieved: he was enjoying his time with this lovely young woman, but he could not quite shake the guilt he was feeling, thinking of Freddie sick and alone while he dined in style at a fashionable Paris bistro. Now it was ending, and he could get back to Freddie.

When the bill arrived, Cailie insisted she pay. "It's my treat," she said. "I was expecting a boring evening all alone in Paris. Then here you are to make things a lot more interesting."

"I'm not sure how interesting I made them," Tree said.

"Would you like to do me a favor?"

"Sure, what can I do?"

"Do you mind if we share a taxi?"

"Of course not." Why wouldn't he share a taxi, after all? At this time of night, it would be hard enough to get one cab, let alone two.

I'm staying at the Lutetia. Do you know where that is?"

"On Boulevard Raspail. I've stayed there many times."

"If you could drop me off, that would be great."

To his surprise, they found a taxi waiting outside—his lucky night for cabs in Paris. They were only five minutes away. They rode in silence down the wide boulevard to the hotel. When they pulled up in front, Cailie said, "This is really embarrassing."

"What is it?" Tree said.

"The fiancé I was telling you about? I broke it off, like I said, but he's followed me to Paris."

"This guy is here?"

She nodded. "That's why I went to La Closerie des Li-las tonight. He was bothering me, so I jumped in a taxi and, not knowing where else to go, I told the driver to take me there. My fiancé doesn't know a whole lot about Paris restaurants, so it worked. Would you mind walking me to my hotel room, just in case he's lurking around."

"Sure," Tree said. "But if he's threatening you, you should go to the police."

"Well, I'm not particularly anxious to deal with the French police, and it's just for tonight. I'm flying back to St. Louis tomorrow. Besides, I've got the Sanibel Sunset detective with me, so I'll be all right."

"I'm not so sure about that," Tree said. "But let's get you inside the hotel."

She insisted on paying the driver. They went up the front entrance steps. The lobby was deserted, no sign of unhappy fiancés. Tree had stayed at the Lutetia during the eighties when it was in its five-star glory. Tonight, the lobby appeared shopworn, a grand dowager still trying to put on a good front, but no longer able to hide the fact that age was catching up with her—a bit like himself.

Tree followed Cailie to the bank of elevators. "I'll say goodbye here," he said.

"Humor me, please, Tree," she said. "Stay with me un-til I get to my room."

"All right," he said. Yes, that was the polite thing to do, he thought. The last few moments in the final act of the production titled *Reliving Your Youth*—making sure the beautiful young woman got safely to her room.

She smiled her thanks. "It's probably nothing. But just in case."

They took the elevator to the sixth floor and stepped into a long corridor done in drab greens and browns. "I was just thinking," she said. "Maybe you'll expand your agency. Soon you'll need another Sanibel Sunset detective."

"Why? Do you have experience as a detective?"

They reached the door to her room. She inserted a card in the lock, and the little light blinked green, and the door clicked open.

"Sanibel Island sounds intriguing."

"It's a unique, lovely island, no question," Tree said.

He held the door for her and she went through saying, "Come in for a moment."

He followed her inside. The door hushed shut behind them. He had an impression of two single beds pushed together—a bad habit at the Lutetia, Tree thought—heavy drapes, French doors open to the cooling night air. Cailie Fisk in a blur descended, wrapping her arms around him, her lips anxious to find his mouth, her slim body pressed hard against him.

He was so taken aback that for a moment he did nothing—the telling, damning, weak moment that was to haunt him. Then, realizing what he was doing, or wasn't doing, he jerked away in the same panicky manner he might have dodged a punch.

"What are you doing?" The words sounded forced and lame.

"It's Paris," she said, curiously out of breath.

She reached around, doing something to her blouse. The next thing, to his astonishment, she was naked to the waist. He backed toward the door, turning away from the glowing invitation of her body.

"What's wrong with you?" she called.

"I'm leaving," he said.

"You're what?" Cailie amazed.

He reached the door. Cailie crossed to him, her face twisting into anger. "You fool," she said. "You stupid fool."

"I thought I was helping you," was all he could think to say.

"Get out," she yelled. "Get out of here!"

He struggled to open the door. She called him more names and then he was outside, the air conditioned silence of the corridor wrapping around him. He took deep breaths, assaulted by conflicting emotions, among them, he had to admit, stirring lust, but also—the detective rising—suspicion. What was a stunning young woman doing coming onto him like that? What was she up to?

He half expected Cailie to come after him. But her door remained closed as he stumbled thankfully into an elevator.

Outside, a sleepy doorman stepped off the curb to flag down a taxi for him. As he waited, it occurred to him that maybe he still held some untapped attraction for women, an allure obscured by marriage and Freddie's overwhelming presence. Let out on his own, women could not resist him. He could hear Freddie's echoing laughter as the doorman held the taxi door for him.

By the time the taxi dropped him off, and he climbed the stairs to the apartment, it was nearly one o'clock, and he was exhausted—tiring work escaping beautiful, predatory women.

Freddie lay curled in the bed, barely visible in the darkness. She did not stir as he finished undressing and eased himself next to her.

He lay there, feeling empty and sick and terribly guilty in Paris.

# 3

Tree should have told his wife.

But he didn't. And that's when the trouble started.

It started on a morning shortly after they got back to Sanibel when his friend Rex Baxter stepped on board the thirty-two foot cabin cruiser, *Former Actor*, he had purchased on eBay, and said, "No one in Paris loves Paris. I've spent enough time in the city to know that much. Only tourists love Paris. Tourists like you, Tree. They hold onto this romantic myth that doesn't exist, except maybe in old movies."

As he talked, Rex turned the ignition on his new boat. The engine coughed a couple of times, but failed to turn over.

Tree Callister stood on the rear deck watching Rex, the president of the Sanibel-Captiva Chamber of Commerce, who had never owned a boat before, and Todd Jackson, who remained dubiously on the dock at the Port Sanibel Marina.

"It's a great boat," Tree said.

"It won't start," Todd said. He was an elegant-looking man with a carefully trimmed mustache who owned and operated Sanibel Biohazard, a company that specialized in cleaning up after dead people.

"It will start," Rex said. He turned the ignition again. This time the engine did not even cough.

"You should never have bought this boat," Todd said.

"It's a great boat," Tree repeated with an enthusiasm he didn't feel. Secretly, he agreed with Todd. Rex was many things, but he was not a boat person.

"It's a great boat, except it won't start," Todd said.

"It will start," Rex insisted.

But it didn't. Rex started swearing.

"I told you," Todd said calmly. "You have bought yourself an ocean of trouble with this tub."

Rex swore some more.

"Don't get mad at me," Todd said. "Get mad at the dude who sold you a boat with an engine that doesn't work."

"It works, it works," Rex insisted, tearing at the hatch cover. The three men stared down at the twin Crusader engines. "It looks all right," Rex said.

"How's it supposed to look?" Todd said.

Rex looked at Tree.

"What I don't understand," he said waving his hand expansively to take in not only the boat but also the Lighthouse Restaurant overlooking the bay, "is how you could ever leave all this. You live in paradise here on Sanibel Island."

"Where you can buy your own boat on eBay that doesn't work," Todd interjected.

"It works," Rex protested. "It works fine."

"It just doesn't start, that's all," Todd said.

"Five hundred thousand visitors every year dream and scrimp and save their money so they can spend time in paradise," Rex said with an angry, frustrated edge to his voice. "So what do you do, Tree? You leave paradise. For Paris? For the smog from all those cars and the smoke from all those Frenchmen puffing on Gauloises? I don't get it. You know what Arthur Frommer, the guide guy, said about this island, don't you?"

"Shouldn't we concentrate on the boat," said Tree in a tired voice, having heard this a thousand times before. "We're standing in the middle of a marina. There must be someone around here who knows what to do."

"Frommer rates Sanibel Island as his top travel destination," Rex continued, undeterred. "Paris came in third. *Third,* behind Sanibel."

"You should be ashamed of yourself, Tree, for even thinking of leaving," Todd said.

"It's his wife," Rex said. "Tree made the mistake of marrying one of those sophisticated, worldly women who can speak French. Naturally, women like that can seduce men into doing anything, even going to Paris."

Tree's cell phone rang. It was so seldom he ever received a call on the phone, it made him jump. "It's okay, Tree," Rex said. "No one's taking a shot at you. It's just your cell phone. They do ring from time to time."

"It's not a cell phone, it's a *smart* phone," Tree said.

"Whoever it is, ask them if they know anything about boats," Todd said.

Tree held his smart phone and said, "Sanibel Sunset Detective Agency, Tree Callister speaking."

"Mr. Callister," an English-accented voice said, "my name is Trembath. Joseph Trembath. I'm executive assistant to Miram Shah. Are you aware who he is?"

"I'm afraid I'm not," Tree said.

"That's fine," Trembath said. "The point is Mr. Shah would like to speak to you. He's over on Useppa Island. We were wondering if it might be possible for you to come over here to have a meeting with him."

"I'm afraid I don't have easy access to a boat."

"We would send a boat for you."

"When would you like to do this?"

"How's your time this afternoon?"

"Sure," Tree said. "I could make some time this afternoon."

"Shall we say two o'clock at the South Seas Resort boat dock?"

"I'll be at there."

"Very good, Mr. Callister. I look forward to seeing you then."

Tree closed his phone. Rex was back at the controls, hitting the ignition switch. Todd was bent over the engines as if he knew something about them. He cocked his head. "I thought I heard a sound," he said.

"What?"

"A slight whirring sound, I think."

Tree said, "Either of you ever heard of someone named Miram Shah?"

They both looked at him blankly. Rex said, "Is that who just called?"

"His assistant. I think he wants to hire me."

"Good," said Rex. "Maybe you'll finally be able to pay the exorbitant rent I charge you."

"Money you'll need to get the boat fixed," Todd said.

"The boat's okay, I tell you. Must be some sort of electrical thing."

"A sea of trouble my friend," Todd said. "A sea of trouble. It's only just started. Don't say I didn't warn you."

"I got no more time for this," Rex said. "I'd better get to the office and finish up my eagerly anticipated newsletter." He grinned at Tree and slapped him on the arm.

"Glad you're back."

"Good to be back—I think. And congratulations on your boat."

"It's going to work fine."

"If you get it fitted with oars," Todd said.

———————

Back in his office upstairs at the Chamber of Commerce Visitors Center, Tree Googled Miram Shah's name. A five-year-old *New York Times* story reported that Miram Shah, the deputy director of Pakistan's Interservice Intelligence Agency—the ISI—was in Washington to meet with American officials aiming to strengthen ties with the agency that was the Pakistani equivalent of America's Central Intelligence Agency.

The *Times* said Shah supported General Zia ul-Haq when he seized power in 1977. That support quickly propelled Shah into the upper echelons of the intelligence community, and brought him into contact with the CIA and its covert operations against the Soviets in neighboring Afghanistan. Shah, according to the *Times*, worked closely with American intelligence and the Afghan Mujahedeen.

Wikipedia picked up Shah's story: when Pervez Musharraf became president, Shah was placed in charge of the ISI's SS Directorate, responsible for covert paramilitary and political operations. Once again, he worked closely with the CIA.

He apparently fell out of favor with the government in 2005 after another *Times* story quoted a Pakistani government official denying that the ISI deputy chief Miram Shah was the mastermind behind several plots to assassinate Afghanistan president Hamid Karzai. Less than a year later, Shah had retired from the ISI, and he had disappeared from the Google search engine.

Now, apparently, the former Pakistani spy was living on Useppa Island.

Tree lifted himself out of his chair and stretched, wondering what he might be getting himself into. What was the former deputy head of Pakistani intelligence doing on Useppa Island? And what could such a high-level international spook possibly want with Tree Callister?

He thought of all this as he stared out the window into the parking lot, filling at the noon hour with tourist SUVs and vans. He watched a Range Rover pull into one of the last empty parking spots. A woman got out and began walking toward the entrance.

Tree couldn't believe it. He was seeing things.

Had to be.

He thumped down the back stairs, startling one of the volunteers who was just getting off the phone. She looked at him questioningly. He ignored her and went through to the main reception area.

Rex Baxter leaned against the counter, holding court, surrounded by a group of adoring visitors.

"You know that Sanibel is Arthur Frommer's favorite destination? He's the famous guide guy. Paris came in third behind Sanibel. *Third.*"

Everyone murmured surprise and approval. Someone said, "Weren't you in *High Sierra* with Humphrey Bogart?" He was referring to the days when Rex was an actor in Hollywood.

"No, no," he said with a laugh. "I'm old but I'm not *that* old. I was in the *remake* of *High Sierra*. It was called *I*

*Died A Thousand Times*. It starred Jack Palance, of all people, in the Bogart role. Shelly Winters was in it, too, and it was all in color this time. I was the kid who befriends Jack. The thing I remember about Jack, he had a funny way of peeling a banana. He didn't actually peel it; he sort of tore it open at the sides, like an animal."

Tree moved past Rex and spotted the woman near the main entrance studying a wall map of Sanibel and Captiva. She was in three-quarter profile, wearing a print blouse tucked into white jeans.

He called out, "Cailie." She didn't respond. He called her name again.

She turned with a confused look on her face. "Are you talking to me?"

"It's Tree," he said. "Tree Callister."

She looked even more confused. "Yes?"

"What are you doing here?"

"What are you talking about? Who are you?"

"Come on," he said quietly, "you know who I am."

"I have no idea who you are," she said.

"You're Cailie. Cailie Fisk."

"I think you've mistaken me for someone else."

Around them, quick glances were being cast in Tree's direction. He stared hard at her. Blonde hair was pulled back in a ponytail and she wore no makeup, but there were those same direct blue eyes and that square, supermodel jaw. It was her. It was Cailie—*had* to be Cailie.

"What are you doing?" he said.

"I think you had better leave me alone," she said.

He watched dumbfounded as she turned and left the center. He followed her as far as the door, ignoring the watching eyes.

Rex stood beside him. "What's going on?" Rex demanded. "Why are you standing there looking so funny?"

"It's nothing," Tree said.

He opened the door and stepped outside onto the ramp leading to the parking lot as the Range Rover reached the exit. If the Rover turned left, then the woman was leaving the island and he had made a mistake and this was going away. If the vehicle turned right, then it would mean she was staying and maybe he had not made a mistake, and this was not going away.

The Range Rover turned right. Tree stood there in the blazing Florida sun, numb and confused. He should have told her. He should have told Freddie. He should have told her everything.

But he didn't. Now he was into this.

# 4

A sea turtle crossing Sanibel-Captiva Drive stopped traffic near the Ding Darling Wildlife Preserve. The turtle was one of the world's oldest creatures, but this afternoon Tree felt much older, still shaken by his encounter with Cailie Fisk. Or with the woman who said she wasn't Cailie Fisk. If it was Cailie, why was she denying it? And what was she doing on Sanibel Island? If the woman wasn't Cailie, then maybe he really was losing it.

The morning after his encounter with Cailie Fisk at La Closerie des Lilas, Freddie had awakened feeling much better. They had spent their last day wandering around, doing some shopping before finally securing a good table at Café Deux Magots for a farewell drink.

He did not say anything about the previous night. When Freddie asked, he said he had taken a taxi over to the Closerie and had escargots and chicken at the bar. Why he lied, even about what he had eaten, he didn't quite know. Perhaps he did not want to admit to himself, let alone to Freddie, that for a moment—just a moment—he might have been tempted by the half-naked Cailie in her Lutetia hotel room. Whatever temptation there was, he had resisted, but the fact that even now he could not quite shake the memory of her in the dim lamplight, disturbed him.

So he said nothing, fearing that if he said anything it would cast a shadow over their marriage that had not been there before and destroy any beneficial effect the week in Paris might have had.

They were home now—back to paradise, as Rex would have it. The good, comfortable life with Freddie had returned to something like normal, insofar as Freddie's uncertainty about her job with Dayton's could be called "normal." And then there was his son and his murky future. Tree didn't want to think about that. He didn't want to think about anything.

The guard in the gatehouse at the South Seas Island Resort waved him through. He parked in the lot and then climbed on one of the resort's trolleys for the ride over to the harbor where Joseph Trembath, as promised, was waiting for him.

Trembath certainly looked British, that is if the proper British male stranded in Florida wore white linen slacks and matching white tennis shoes, and possessed merry green eyes that twinkled against a tanned face, framed by iron gray hair and set off by a military-type mustache. Tree was certain the mustache could be made to bristle on command.

Trembath greeted him with an enthusiasm that matched his handshake. "A great pleasure. I do appreciate you coming out on such short notice and so does Mr. Shah, I'm bound to say."

"Well, I'm certainly interested in why Mr. Shah would want to meet with me," Tree said.

Trembath made his green eyes dance. "Let's find out, shall we? Mr. Shah is waiting for us."

He led Tree over to dockside where a sleek thirty-four foot Cobalt was moored. A dark-haired young man, almost as sleek as the boat, waited at the wheel. Trembath stepped from the dock onto the rear deck and Tree followed.

"Would you like something to drink, old chap?" Trembath asked. *Old chap?* Tree thought. It had been a long time since anyone called him "old chap," and the first time anyone had ever addressed him that way in Florida.

"I'm fine, thanks," Tree said.

"All right, then Jim," he said to the young driver. "Let's be off."

Jim turned on the ignition and started up the twin engines while Trembath undid the lines. Minutes later they were crashing over white caps and turning north into Pine Island Sound.

Tree sat with Trembath in the back. Trembath folded his arms and lifted his head high, his mouth twisted into a rictus grin, as though mounting a defense against the whipping wind.

Tree leaned toward his ear and asked, "Have you worked for Mr. Shah long?"

"The wind, can't hear a thing, old chap," Trembath yelled back at Tree's ear. "Let's wait till we're on shore. We'll talk then."

Fifteen minutes later, they passed Cabbage Key and the outlines of Useppa Island came into view. The island remained best known for its role in the ill-fated 1960 Bay of Pigs invasion when the Central Intelligence Agency used it to train anti-Castro fighters. Today, it still managed to cling to its status as a private island requiring membership to live there. Its website urged only the most exclusive travelers to inquire about membership. Translated into plain English: you better be pretty darned rich if you want to live here. Tree expected Captain Jim to land his craft at the marina adjacent to the Collier Inn. Instead, he slowed the boat and turned south toward a long, narrow dock jutting into the bay. Closer, Captain Jim cut the motor and the boat drifted smartly into the dock where two trim young men grabbed the ropes Jim and Trembath threw them. Soon the boat was tied off, and Tree clambered onto the dock.

"Welcome, sir," one of the young men said with a grin. "I'm Benedict. My friend here is Mark."

"How do you do, sir?" Mark said in an accent as plummy as his friend's.

"Do you mind if I pat you down?" Benedict asked.

"What?"

"Security, old chap," Trembath said, smoothing his wind-ruffled hair. "You know how things are these days."

"They're so bad you have to be frisked on Useppa Island?"

Trembath shrugged helplessly. "Only takes a minute, old chap."

In his cheap khaki slacks and imitation Polo shirt, Tree wasn't sure where he would ever hide a gun, but he lifted his arms out and Benedict quickly patted him down.

"Thanks very much, sir," Benedict said when he finished.

"We appreciate your co-operation," said Mark.

"Come along, Mr. Callister," Trembath said. "Mr. Shah isn't far away."

Trembath led him off the dock across an expanse of lawn to a row of two-story wood-frame houses surrounded by wide porches. They started up the steps of the house directly in front of them.

As they came onto the porch, a slim, barefoot old man with walnut-colored skin used a cane to heave himself out of a wicker chair. He wore a white linen shirt and white trousers. The man in white, Tree thought. He looked nothing like someone Tree might imagine to be in charge of Pakistani spying. But then spies weren't supposed to look like spies, were they?

"There you are, Mr. Shah," Trembath said. "I would like you to meet Mr. Tree Callister. Mr. Callister, this is Mr. Miram Shah."

"It is such a pleasure, Mr. Callister." Miram Shah spoke in a formal, lightly accented voice. The two men shook hands. "Thank you for coming all this way to see an old man. Can we get you something to drink after your journey?"

"If you have some sparkling water," Tree said.

Magically, a houseman, also ancient and also in white, appeared. Tree took note of the white gloves he wore. Miram Shah spoke rapidly in a language Tree didn't understand. The houseman in the white gloves bowed slightly and then went back into the house.

"You don't mind sitting out here, do you Mr. Callister?"

"Not at all."

"It's so pleasant at this time of day. At any time of the day, really. Are you familiar with the island?"

"I was here with my wife when we first moved to Captiva," Tree said as he followed Miram Shah over to where four wicker armchairs were grouped facing one another around a glass-topped table.

Leaning heavily on his cane, Shah eased himself onto the cushions of the chair facing away from the sea. Tree sat opposite him with a view of the water and pleasure craft throwing off silver wakes as they made their way toward the marina at the Collier Inn. Trembath, Tree noticed, perched in the wicker chair midway between himself and Shah, the referee for this afternoon's encounter.

"I love it here," Miram Shah said as he settled into the chair. "I love the sunshine of course, but also the peace and serenity."

"Does your own country not provide similar peace and serenity?" Tree asked, curious as to what Shah might reveal about where he came from.

Shah smiled vaguely and said, "Ah, here we go," an instant before the houseman reappeared carrying a silver tray upon which was set a single tall glass of sparkling water. The houseman presented the glass to Tree, bowed slightly, and left. A breeze roused the wind chimes at the end of the porch.

Trembath leaned forward and said, "Mr. Shah has asked you here today, Mr. Callister, in regards to a matter requiring utmost discretion."

He paused to give Tree a chance to reply. Tree had no idea what to say, so he just looked at Trembath who cleared his throat and sat back, his gaze turning to Shah—the signal for the old man to speak.

"It is my fiancée, Mr. Callister," he said.

Tree said, "Yes," as though everyone's fiancée was a problem.

"Two days ago, she left the house, and hasn't returned," Trembath said. As he spoke, Shah looked pained, and seemed to grip his cane more firmly.

"Do you have any idea where she might have gone?" Tree looked at Shah when he asked the question.

Shah shook his head, but it was Trembath who said, "That's what we would like you to find out."

When Tree remained unexpectedly silent, Trembath added, "Discreetly of course. This is a highly embarrassing situation. Mr. Shah would not want it to be made public."

Which begged the question why the public might be interested in Mr. Shah's relationship problems. Instead of asking, Tree said, "Mr. Shah, why did your fiancée leave?"

"What difference does that make?" Trembath sounded cross.

"Well, if she left to get a loaf of bread and never came back, that's one thing. If she left because she and Mr. Shah had a fight, then that's something else again."

Shah's fist opened and closed on the handle of the cane, as if to express his tense emotional state. "There was a misunderstanding," he said softly. "As a result of that misunderstanding, Elizabeth left."

"Elizabeth?" Tree said.

"Elizabeth Traven," Trembath said. "The woman in question is Elizabeth Traven."

# 5

Is everything all right, Mr. Callister?" A concerned expression had popped onto Trembath's placid face.

How could he answer that? Nothing was ever all right as far as Elizabeth Traven was concerned. She haunted his life, the darkly beautiful specter he could never quite shake, even on Useppa Island, talking to elderly Pakistani spies. Wherever he went, Elizabeth somehow managed to reinsert herself into his life. He was, as he usually was with her, at once appalled—and intrigued.

Tree managed to say, "You are engaged to marry Elizabeth Traven, Mr. Shah?"

Shah nodded and said, "Yes."

Trembath studied Tree carefully before he said, "We understand you know Mrs. Traven."

"I've done work for Elizabeth Traven." An understatement if there ever was one.

The light lit Shah's face. "Very satisfactory work, I understand. That is why Elizabeth recommended you."

"She recommended that you hire me to find her?"

Shah allowed a tiny smile. "No, no, we were discussing you in connection with another matter. She thought you might be appropriate should we have needed to make certain inquiries."

"What kind of inquiries?"

Shah seemed not to hear the question.

Trembath leaned further forward as if fearful he was being left out of the conversation. "It occurred to Mr. Shah and me that because you know Mrs. Traven, it might be appropriate for you to act as an intermediary."

"In order to do what?"

"To find her, of course." Trembath said this in a way that suggested you would have to be an idiot not to know that.

"And then what?" Tree addressed Shah: "You want me to convince her to come back?"

"Yes, give it a shot, old chap," Trembath said, as if he was an officer in some British World War II adventure— Jack Hawkins sending the team of saboteurs off on an impossible mission.

"You must tell me, Mr. Callister, what are you rates?" Shah accompanied the question with a thin smile, as though talking about money pained him.

"I charge two hundred dollars a day, plus expenses."

"Mr. Callister, it has been a great pleasure to meet you." Shah abruptly gripped the cane with both hands to pull himself to his feet.

"Hold on, Mr. Shah," Tree said.

"Yes?" Shah looked surprised anyone would attempt to interrupt his departure.

"Are you hiring me or is this your way of telling me the price is too high?"

Trembath frowned. "Your fee is not an issue, Mr. Callister."

"Then if I am hired, I'm going to need more information."

A frown similar to Trembath's now crossed Miram Shah's face. "What sort of information?"

"When was the last time you saw Elizabeth?"

He paused to consider this before he said, "One week ago."

"Where did you last see her?"

"She was here."

"And she seemed all right?"

"She seemed fine."

"You said there was a misunderstanding. Did you have an argument, some sort of altercation? Something that would make her suddenly disappear?"

"No," he said, uneasily, as if this topic of conversation was disturbing to him.

Trembath leaned forward again. "This is not easy for Mr. Shah. I can provide any further information you might require."

Shah forced another tiny smile. "I am certain you will do a fine job for us, Mr. Callister. I will leave it to you and Mr. Trembath to conclude the agreement."

Tree and Trembath stood together as Shah, leaning on his cane, hobbled away. Tree turned to Trembath and said, "What's going on here?"

"I suggest we get something a little stronger, what do you say to that, old chap?"

As though that was his cue, the houseman in the white gloves reappeared. Trembath said, "Chandio, bring me the strongbox and a gin and tonic, like a good fellow." It was not hard to imagine Trembath in uniform ordering the servants around during the British Raj. From the look on his face, Chandio didn't have any trouble imagining it, either.

"What about you, Callister? Will you take something?"

"Nothing except the answer to my question."

Trembath frowned. "What question was that?"

"The question that went like this: what's going on here?"

"Simple enough, old chap. Mr. Shah would like you to locate his fiancée, Elizabeth Traven, find out what the situation is, and persuade her to come back."

"Persuade her to come back to Shah?"

"If it's possible, yes."

"Why would you think I have any chance of persuading Elizabeth to do anything?"

"Well, I don't have to think, do I? It's Mr. Shah who has to do that, and for whatever reason, he apparently believes your previous association with Mrs. Traven can be of assistance. What's more, he's going to pay you enough money so that you will think so, too."

"I know something of his background," Tree said.

"Do you?" Trembath sounded surprised.

"Miram Shah either is or was the deputy head of Pakistani security. I gather he has spent a fair amount of time in Washington interacting with the CIA. But you don't sound like CIA to me, Mr. Trembath."

He barked out a laugh. "No, no, definitely not CIA. British Intelligence a world ago. MI-6."

"That's what? Britain's external intelligence service?"

"Correct. More formally known as the Secret Intelligence Service. I was assigned to Islamabad ten years ago, liaising with the then-deputy chief's staff. That's how I got to know Miram. When he retired, he persuaded me to go along with him and provide security."

"And help find lost girlfriends?"

Trembath took the jibe in stride. "Let's just say the job comes with unexpected demands."

"What's he doing on Useppa Island?"

"Why, this is where he lives, Mr. Callister. He's fallen in love with your wonderful country, and one of your wondrous women, and now you can help him find her."

"What do you think, Mr. Trembath? Any idea what's happened to Elizabeth?"

"I'm afraid I don't, old chap. I've been pretty much kept out of the loop on this whole matter."

Chandio re-emerged from the house, carrying the gin and tonic in one white gloved hand and a gray-metal strongbox in the other. He handed the gin to Trembath and then placed the box on the glass-topped table. "Ah, here we are," Trembath said, taking a long sip from his drink.

Chandio stepped away, standing casually at attention as Trembath opened the strong box to reveal stacks of hundred dollar bills that looked as though Chandio had just run them off a printing press in the house. Trembath grabbed at a wad of bills as if he planned to disperse them to the egrets flying past. Instead, he quickly counted out a pile of hundreds and offered them to Tree. "There's three thousand dollars to get you started."

Tree looked at the money in Trembath's hand and said, "I'm not sure what I can do."

Trembath just smiled. "Why don't we find out?"

Tree took the money. He noticed Chandio. His sober face was devoid of expression. His black eyes, however, filled with a combination of fire and disdain for these duplicitous westerners.

# 6

On the trip back, Tree kept his eyes focused on Captain Jim's back, while marveling how he once again had allowed himself to be talked into getting tangled up with Elizabeth Traven.

A former journalist before she married the now-deceased media mogul Brand Traven, Elizabeth had written biographies of Lenin and Trotsky. But inside the writer, beat the heart of a conniving, manipulative liar who could never, never be trusted.

The mask of her beauty allowed Elizabeth to get away with, literally, in Freddie's estimation, murder. She accused Tree of being like most of the men Elizabeth encountered, totally infatuated, and thus blind to her devious nature.

Tree hotly denied this, even as he knew that as part of Elizabeth's seemingly endless campaign to twist him around her little finger, she had once awkwardly attempted to seduce him. The memory of that night lingered, no question, but that did not stop him from protesting loudly that he was not attracted to Elizabeth Traven—he loved his wife too much—and even if he was, he was too smart to ever get mixed up with her again. Yet try as he might he could not—or would not—resist the temptation. Was it the money? That's what he would tell himself. But maybe something else as well, a strange alchemy that inevitably drew him to her. Plain curiosity, too, he supposed—what the devil was Elizabeth up to now?

He drove south away from the South Seas Island Resort after Captain Jim dropped him off, deciding that since Elizabeth's house on Captiva Drive was nearby, he would stop by for a visit, and perhaps get some understanding of what this was all about.

Was she really planning to marry the former head of Pakistani security? With a former spy from MI-6 as best man? It didn't seem very likely; there had to be something else at play here.

But what?

The great stone Captiva Drive monstrosity that was Elizabeth Traven's sun-splashed lair stood behind a high wall and locked gates, giving no hint anyone ever lived there. It seemed to be on perfect permanent display, evidence of what the American dream, Florida division, might provide the outsized dreamer.

He tried the intercom. No one answered. So much for a quick end to this case, a fast resolution of innate curiosity. He had already taken Miram Shah's money. He would have to find Elizabeth Traven.

Now how was he going to do that?

———

The house Freddie and Tree had purchased on Andy Rosse Lane was mounted on stilts, protection against the hurricanes that always threatened paradise. The house was their pride and joy. Freddie's car was already parked in the drive. He found her in the kitchen, having changed from work clothes into her evening uniform— shorts and a T-shirt—pouring the one glass of chardonnay she allowed herself after work.

"You're home early," he said kissing her.

She finished pouring the wine and said, "Come on, let's sit outside."

"Is everything all right?"

"I'm not sure," she said.

They sat on the terrace as they did most evenings. Not far away he could hear the pleasurable yelps from tourists gathered outside the Mucky Duck for the daily ritual of the setting sun, the tourists praying to the gods for cheaper beer and better weather. The gods usually acted on the weather; not so much on the cheap beer.

Freddie stretched her wonderfully long legs and issued a deep sigh before she said, "I met with Vera this afternoon." Ever since they returned from Paris, Ray Dayton's widow had been keeping everyone up in the air as to her intentions for the five Dayton's supermarkets located throughout the Lee and Collier County area, including the store on Sanibel Island.

"She says she is seriously considering selling the business."

"I guess that's not too surprising. Vera never struck me as the kind of person who wants to run a chain of supermarkets. Any idea who she would sell it to?"

"She might sell it to me," Freddie said.

"Whoa, hold on there a minute. Are you seriously thinking of buying Dayton's?"

"You don't think I can?"

"Can you?"

"Let's put it this way: there appears to be real interest from my people in Chicago."

"You have people in Chicago?"

"Investors I've worked with in the past."

"You would *own* Dayton's?"

"I wouldn't own it, exactly, but I would head a syndicate that would purchase the five stores in the chain, yes."

"I guess I shouldn't be surprised," he said, even though he was. "I mean, if anyone could pull off something like this, it's my wife."

"Well, thanks for that vote of confidence, but it is all in the very early talking stage," Freddie said. "Vera is all over the place. One day she wants me there, the next she doesn't. One day she wants to sell; the next she's thinking about hanging on."

Tree sat there taking all this in.

"The silence," she said. "What does that mean?"

"It doesn't mean anything. I'm excited for you. I hope it happens."

Did he really mean that? He wasn't certain. At moments like this Tree realized just how far away he was from the world in which Freddie operated. He wondered what the reaction would be if he went to Chicago looking for enough money to buy a chain of supermarkets. He wouldn't even know whom to ask. Freddie did. That was the difference.

She sipped at her wine, and said, "Tell me about your day."

"Rex has a new boat, and, of course, can't get the engine started."

"Of course."

"I've got a new client."

Freddie raised her eyebrows to encourage him to go on.

"The former head of Pakistani Interservice. Apparently, it's the Pakistani equivalent of the CIA. His name is Miram Shah."

"The former head of the Pakistani secret service is here?"

"He's living on Useppa Island. They took me out there by boat this afternoon to meet him. He wants me to work for him."

"To do what?"

"To find his missing fiancée."

"Okay."

"You're not going to believe who his fiancée is."

"Try me," Freddie said.

"He says he's engaged to Elizabeth Traven."

Freddie's face darkened perceptibly. "Elizabeth Traven is going to marry a Pakistani spy? I don't believe it."

"After I got back from Useppa, I dropped around to her place."

"Oh, great," Freddie said.

"She wasn't there. The gate was locked. The place looked deserted."

"And you're going to do this? You're going to try to find her?"

"What would you say if I said yes?"

She rose and came over and bent to kiss his mouth. "Tree, my darling, Tree, we are getting too old for this. I am sixty now, remember?"

"That's impossible," Tree said. "I know that's what you told me in Paris in order to lure me into bed with you."

"If I was trying to lure you, I wouldn't tell you I was sixty."

"You're lying through your teeth."

"Nonetheless, we could be on the verge of, financially, not having to worry about anything. I don't want to spend the rest of whatever life I've got left wondering whether my husband is coming home."

"I always come home," Tree said.

"This from a guy who no sooner became a private detective than he got himself shot."

"It was a couple of weeks at least."

"Who was almost dinner for two alligators."

"I knew I shouldn't have told you about that."

"And not so long ago lost most of his front teeth in a beating."

"But the point is, I survived the gunshot wound. The alligators didn't eat me, and I've got lovely new teeth that make me look like Brad Pitt."

"No, the point is, you've been very lucky. But one of these days your luck is going to run out."

"It's going to run out for all of us," Tree said. "It's how you live until you die. That's what makes the difference."

"You've been reading Hemingway again."

That reduced them both to silence.

"To tell you the truth, I'm worried about Elizabeth," Tree said finally. "What's she doing mixed up with spies?"

"It's not worry," Freddie said. "The correct term is obsession."

"No, it's not. I didn't look these people up. They came to me."

"But how do you think they got your name, Tree?"

"They say they got it from Elizabeth," Tree said.

"Why is she giving them your name? And if this guy really is a spy, why does he need you? Doesn't he know other agents who could find Elizabeth? And I don't believe Elizabeth was about to marry some Pakistani spy and then, like some fluttery Tennessee Williams heroine, ran away at the last moment."

"Do Tennessee Williams heroines run away?"

"Blanche DuBois did. How do you think she ended up in New Orleans?"

"Elizabeth is no Blanche."

"She's up to something, and that can only mean trouble for you. I don't want to tell you what to do, but I would stay as far away from this as you possibly can."

"I'm going to make a couple of phone calls, that's all," Tree said. "Besides, I've already taken their money. Three thousand dollars."

Freddie shook her head in feigned exasperation—or maybe not so feigned. "I'm going in to make us some dinner."

"Are you mad at me?"

"I'm worried about you."

"I keep telling you, Freddie. There's nothing to worry about." Was there? Well, actually there probably was, but not tonight.

"So if I told you that since we got back from Paris, you don't seem the same, what would you say?"

"I would say that Paris wasn't Paris this time—for either of us."

"No," Freddie said evenly. "I don't suppose it was."

She gave him a fleeting look and then went into the house.

# 7

On his way down Captiva Drive the following morning, Tree again stopped by the Traven mansion. The gates remained locked tight. He tried Elizabeth's cell phone. It rang a dozen times. No one answered. The call did not go into voice mail.

When he got to the office, he sat for a few more minutes thinking about Cailie—kicking himself for not telling Freddie about her. He actually contemplated phoning her at work. But then what was he going to say? "Hi, honey. Incidentally, I forgot to tell you. The week we went to Paris to celebrate your birthday? I went out, met another woman, had dinner with her, and then went back to her hotel room where she bared her breasts and kissed me. I didn't do anything, of course—except not tell you about it until now. And I'm only telling you now because I think she's shown up on Sanibel."

No, he decided, that was not the phone call he was going to make this morning.

His reverie was interrupted by the arrival of a tall, heavyset man with an impressive head of curly white hair.

He leaned in the doorway and pointed a sausage-like finger at Tree. "You the detective?"

Tree looked at him. "Who are you looking for?"

"They said downstairs, you, the detective. Upstairs. Is that right?"

"I'm Tree Callister, I run the Sanibel Sunset Detective Agency."

The man ventured further into the room. He wore a loose, collarless shirt that did little to hide the belly drooping over his khaki cargo shorts. His flip-flops barely contained feet the size of small boats. His toenails badly needed clipping, Tree noticed.

"I am Javor Zoran," he announced. As though that explained everything.

"Mr. Zoran," Tree said. "Take a seat, please. What can I do for you?"

Instead, of moving to the visitors' chair, Zoran placed thick fists on either hip, as if preparing to engage Tree in a fight to the death.

"Tell me, how much you charge for this detecting?"

"Look, first of all, why don't you sit down? If I can help you, then we can discuss price."

Javor Zoran eased himself gingerly into the chair in front of Tree's desk. Once settled, he looked carefully around him, concentrating on the doorway.

"You are going to leave door open?"

"Do you want me to close it?"

"I do not want anyone overhearing us," Zoran said.

Tree got up to shut the door. "Is that better?"

Zoran seemed to think it was. Tree reseated himself and looked expectantly at his visitor.

"Okay," pronounced Zoran. "Here is the thing. You are detective, I need detective to find missing person."

"What missing person is that?"

"A friend is missing person."

"Have you contacted the police?"

The idea appeared to horrify Zoran. "The police? Why would I talk to police?"

"Because they are the people best equipped to find missing persons."

"I come to you to find missing person. And you tell me to go to the police? What kind of detective is that?"

"I'm merely making you aware of your options, Mr. Zoran."

"No, no police. I want discretion. You can give me this, Mister Detective Callister? This discretion?"

"I can certainly be discreet," Tree said. "When did you last see your friend?"

"One week ago."

"Where? Where did you last see this person? Here on Sanibel?"

"No, no. Not Sanibel. Key West. We were in Key West. You must go to Key West and find her."

"Her—this is a woman I'm looking for?"

"Yes, of course. Only a woman can give a man trouble like this."

"You think she's still there? Still in Key West?"

"No, I tell you to go to Key West because she is gone, and I pull a big joke on you." He glowered across the desk. "You are not dumb detective, are you Mr. Callister?"

"Whatever I am, I'm going to need more information than I currently have, Mr. Zoran. What makes you so certain this person is missing?"

"Okay, we go to Key West one week ago. We have great time together. This is a woman with whom I am very much in love. This woman change my life. I have had many women, but no one like this woman. The week comes to an end. I drive to Miami. Business. Three days ago, I am back on the island, on Sanibel. I phone her. No answer. I go to her place. It is locked up. No sign of her. She has disappeared into the air."

Zoran slumped forlornly in his chair: the lover confused and hurt. "I don't know what to do. How many detectives on this island? Only one I can find. You. So I come to you. You go to Key West, and you find her."

"You think she's still in Key West?"

"She is not here."

"Okay. I'll need a name and a photo," Tree said. "And any other information you have on your friend."

"You want photo, Mister Detective Callister? I give you photo." He reached into his pocket and pulled out a four-by-six photograph and handed it to Tree. Zoran, his big gut folding over his swimming trunks, posed on a Key West beach with a woman in a bright red bathing suit. The woman was wearing sunglasses. Tree looked at the photo and then looked at it again. No. It couldn't be.

He glanced up at Zoran. "Tell me who this is," he said.

"Her name is Elizabeth Traven," Zoran said.

Tree shook his head. Was he really hearing this?

"What is wrong with you?" Zoran demanded.

Tree threw the photograph onto the desk. "Who are you, Mr. Zoran?"

"I am most valuable of things." He reached into his pocket again and this time produced a wad of one hundred dollar bills that he threw on top of the photograph.

"I am a customer. You go to Key West, Mr. Callister. You find my Elizabeth. You will find out why she disappears like this. Maybe she no longer wants me, I don't know. You will find out. If you do not want to do this, then you will discover something else about me."

"And what is that, Mr. Zoran?"

"It is not a good thing to disappoint me," he said. "It is not a good thing."

"That's not a threat, is it Mr. Zoran?"

"How could you imagine such a thing?"

"Because I'd hate to start off a relationship with the client threatening me."

"You find my Elizabeth." Zoran said it like it was a marching order.

"When you were in Key West, where did you and Elizabeth stay?"

"A hotel. The Southernmost. You know it?"

Tree nodded. "How do I get in touch with you?"

Zoran stood and for the first time since he entered the office, he smiled. It was not a nice smile.

"I will contact you, Mister Detective Callister."

# 8

According to the Google search engine, Javor Zoran was once in charge of Serbian president Slobodan Milošević's personal security detail. After Milošević's arrest, Zoran had been investigated by the International Criminal Tribunal in The Hague. Prosecutors decided there was not enough evidence to bring him to trial; a decision *The Washington Post* said defied credulity.

There was little doubt Zoran had ordered the deaths of dozens of civilians. The question of prosecuting him hung on whether those murders were committed on such a widespread and systemic basis as to constitute a crime against humanity. The prosecutors at The Hague had concluded they did not. Therefore, Zoran was allowed to go free—a travesty, the *Post* said.

A *Time* magazine story speculated that during his time with Milošević, Zoran was being paid by the CIA. That would help explain, said the magazine, why no charges had been brought against him. The piece suggested he had emigrated to the U.S. with the help of the spy agency.

Tree picked up the photograph of Zoran with Elizabeth Traven. If he hadn't been holding the photo in his hand, he would not have believed it: a Pakistani spy and a Serbian war criminal. How did she get mixed up with these characters? He immediately felt ridiculous for even asking the question. It was Elizabeth. The possibilities for trouble were beyond imagining.

But why had she disappeared? To get herself out of the mess she found herself in? It was certainly a possibility. Thus he had to confront the obvious question: if he found Elizabeth, was he putting her life in danger? More to the point, was he putting his own life in danger?

Two distinct possibilities.

———

Tree got over to the Sanibel Island Holiday Inn a little past noon. When he entered the lobby, his son Chris was just coming out from behind the reception desk, reminding Tree once again of how much he looked like his mother. He had married Judy—the first of four wives, a number even he had trouble believing— when they were both in their early twenties. He should never have done it, they were both far too young—at least Tree was and too much of a newspaperman to want the sort of traditional marriage Judy had in mind. They had produced two sons, Raymond and Chris.

Raymond, the eldest, was a lawyer in Chicago and although he remained close to his mother, Tree had not spoken to him in years. No fights or anything, merely a broken family drifting farther apart. Tree kept meaning to do something about that. But the fact is he didn't do anything.

Chris had lost weight recently, regaining the lean and lanky look that was his trademark before he met his *Playboy* model wife, Kendra. In a lightweight summer suit, he appeared healthier than Tree had seen him in a long time. Chris adjusted his glasses when he saw his father approaching. "What brings you here?"

He didn't sound all that happy to see him, Tree thought.

"I thought I'd drop by and see how you are doing." Tree hugged his son, feeling his back stiffen. Chris didn't like his fatherly display of affection. Tough. He was going to get it, anyway.

"I was just about to go on break. You feel like a cup of coffee?"

"Sure," Tree said.

They crossed the lobby to the restaurant where an impressive faux Banyan tree sprouted out of the floor, its branches spreading across the ceiling. Tree sat at a table while Chris went away and came back with two steaming mugs. Tree watched him with a mixture of love and despair. Chris had always been the problematic son, the silent, enigmatic kid most wounded by his parents' divorce, left adrift in a world that did not seem to interest him very much. He had no passion for journalism that was for sure. If anything, he disdained the profession. It was, after all, the business that employed his disliked father. He was going to go to university. And then he wasn't. Then he enrolled in business at the University of Chicago Booth School of Business—but then didn't attend classes. He had a thousand excuses for his behavior, all of them, Tree was certain, masking resentment of his father and the way he had treated—or rather mistreated— Judy and the boys, charges to which Tree could only plead guilty.

And then Chris had met the beautiful Kendra, siren of desire, celebrated in the pages of *Playboy*, no less. Everyone wanted Kendra, only Chris had her—or sort of had her, as it turned out— and the next thing they were married during a whirlwind weekend in Las Vegas, no family members present, thanks very much. The next thing after that, Kendra and Chris were starting up, of all the curious things, an online dating service, using, Tree believed, money invested by Judy who, since her divorce from Tree, had blossomed into a successful real estate agent in the Oak Park area.

Everything was going to be all right after that. Everything was going to be just fine.

Only it wasn't.

"Just milk, isn't it, Dad?"

"How's the job going?" Tree asked, snapping himself out of his reverie.

"Fine." Chris put the mug down and sat back, looking at his father. "The staff here is great, very pleasant."

"So no problems?"

Chris's smile erased the tension from his face. "To tell you the truth, Dad, it's just the opposite. I've met someone."

"You mean a girl?"

Chris's smile widened. "A young woman, yes."

"You met her here on the island?"

"A couple of months ago. She was a guest at the hotel. You know, we just started talking, nothing serious or anything. Then she went away on a business trip, but now she's back, and I've got to say, things are moving along nicely."

"Have you spoken to Edith Goldman lately?" Edith was Chris's lawyer.

"What? I should call Edith before I date someone?"

"No, of course not. That isn't what I was getting at."

"What are you getting at?"

"I just don't want you to lose sight of the fact you're not out of the woods yet."

"What woods are we talking about?" There was an angry edge to his voice. "What would you like me to do? Sit in my little apartment, fingers crossed, hoping nobody shows up at the door with a warrant for my arrest?"

"No one is saying that."

"Then what are you saying?"

"Look, you are innocent. I know you are."

Chris raised his eyes from the coffee. Haunted eyes, Tree thought. "But that's the dirty little secret here, isn't it, Dad? I *was* there that night. I *could* have killed my wife."

He glared at his father. "Maybe I'm not as innocent as you think."

"Talking like that is not helpful, Chris," Tree said.

Chris waved his hand, as though to clear away the damning words. "Never mind. It's nothing. Me being crazy, I guess."

"Look, it hasn't been that long since Kendra's murder, that's all I'm saying. It might be a little soon to get involved in another relationship."

"What do you think, Dad? Do you think I loved Kendra?" The glittery challenge was back in Chris's eyes; radiating that defiance he had seen so often over the years.

"I don't know, Chris. You tell me. Did you love her?"

"Whether I did or didn't doesn't matter much at this point, does it? The fact is my wife is gone, and I've got to somehow get past it. This woman I've met, maybe she can help me do that."

"Just do me a favor, will you? Call Edith, see if she knows anything."

"Okay."

"In the meantime, if the police come around, for any reason, don't talk to them. Call Edith."

Chris said, "I'll bring her to the Lighthouse, maybe this Friday so you can meet her."

"Meet who?"

He grinned. "Susan. The girl of my dreams."

# 9

"You've got a visitor," Rex said to Tree when he got back to the office.

"Man or a woman?"

"Definitely male."

"What's he look like?"

"Like he wants to kill someone," Rex said.

"Thanks," Tree said. "That's very reassuring."

He started up the stairs.

"Try not to get blood on the carpet," Rex called.

The African-American male sprawled in the visitors' chair certainly looked formidable. His head was shaved, and a permanent scowl was built into a face emblazoned with three diagonal scars slashing his forehead and right cheek, dominated by eyes the size of searchlights that inspected Tree with ill-disguised hostility.

He stroked at a carefully trimmed goatee before he leaned forward and placed a single orange flower on the desk.

"A Calla lily," he said. "A beautiful flower. Yes? I bring this flower to you in friendship."

"That's good to know," Tree said.

The man sat back, eyeing the lily with apparent satisfaction. "Now you must tell me where I can find a good macaron on the island."

"I beg your pardon?"

"A macaron," he said in a high-pitched voice, all wrong for his size; a big man with a small voice. "They are delicate cookie-type confections, made with meringue and egg whites. They are filled with jam or buttercream or ganache. Absolutely delicious. I discovered them in Paris. Everywhere I go I test the local macarons. I did find good macarons in Toronto a few years ago. But so far nothing compares to the macarons of Paris."

"I'm afraid you may be out of luck on the island as far as macarons are concerned."

"This is most disappointing because this is a beautiful place. Sad they don't make macarons here."

Tree squeezed around the visitor and got behind his desk, feeling safer with a barrier separating them.

The visitor wore a gray suit with narrow blue pinstripes and a crisp white shirt and a bright red tie like a trail of blood. A formally dressed thug with a flower, Tree thought.

"Ganache," he said.

"Tree looked at him. "What?"

"Ganache. I always say that ganache is one of the fillings in a macaron. But I never know what it is. Do you know what ganache is?"

"I have no idea," Tree said.

"Ganache." The word rolled smoothly off his tongue. He seemed to savor it. "I must find out what it means."

He added matter-of-factly, "Now I bring the lily in friendship, as I said, because that is the sort of person I am. But I must show you something else." He opened his suit jacket to reveal a shoulder harness from which hung a leather holster-like sheath with a thick wooden handle protruding from it. He pulled the object out of the sheath, revealing a long, gleaming blade.

He laid the blade on the desk beside the lily.

"Know what that is?" the visitor asked.

"It looks like a machete," Tree said.

The visitor nodded with satisfaction. "Where I come from, it is known as a cutlass. A tool useful for taking care of enemies."

He held the flower in one hand. "A flower for my friends." With his other hand, he raised the cutlass. "The cutlass for my enemies."

The man with the shaved head and the scarred face replaced the cutlass blade on the desk and almost daintily touched it with a manicured fingernail. "Here is the thing. I don't want you as my enemy. Okay? I bring you a lily. I don't want to have to use this on you."

Tree found he was having difficulty swallowing. He said, "How can I avoid being your enemy?"

"You avoid being my enemy by being my friend."

"And how do I become your friend?"

"By telling me, very precisely, the whereabouts of Mrs. Elizabeth Traven."

"You can't be serious," Tree said.

"When I am making jokes, my friend, I do not show my cutlass."

"What would make you think I know where she is?"

"Because I am smart about these things. Because I know you have been hired by certain disreputable people to find her. So tell me where she is. Or I will give you short sleeves."

"Short sleeves?"

"In my place, that is what we say when we cut off your hands."

"You're threatening to cut off my hands?"

"Which would make it impossible for you to hold the lily, and that would be very sad."

Tree said as calmly as he could, "It would be helpful if I knew who was threatening me."

The visitor frowned, stroking his goatee again. "You want to know who I am?"

"Yes."

"I already told you."

"No, you didn't."

"I didn't tell you?"

"So far it's been macarons and threats with a machete."

"A cutlass. It's a cutlass."

"Yes. Okay. But I still don't know your name."

My name is Dr. Edgar. Dr. Edgar Bunya."

"Okay, Edgar, tell me why you are so interested in Elizabeth Traven."

"Please. Call me Dr. Bunya."

"Dr. Bunya. Why are you interested in Elizabeth Traven?"

"*That* is none of your business."

"Well, then, we're kind of at an impasse, aren't we? I don't know where she is. You won't tell me why you want to find her."

He lurched to his feet and leaned across the desk to retrieve the cutlass, causing Tree to flinch. That produced what passed for a smile on Edgar Bunya's hard, scarred face. "See," he said. "You are afraid of me. A good thing. As soon as you find Mrs. Traven, you tell me. Understand?"

"How am I supposed to contact you?"

He picked up the lily and Tree saw the slip of paper twisted around its stem. Bunya pointed at it. "That is the number where you can reach me. Call me. Leave a message. As soon as you find her, do it."

He dropped the flower onto the desk and slipped the blade back into its holster before closing his suit jacket over it. Then he turned on his heel and went out the door without another word.

———————

Nothing came up on Google for Edgar Bunya, even after Tree added "doctor" to his search. Then he typed in "short sleeves," and that gave him a lot of fashion stuff about short-sleeved blouses. When he added "cutting off hands," however, that yielded a *London Times* story about rebels of the Revolutionary United Front in Sierra Leone. "Long sleeves" meant they cut off your arm at the elbow. With "short sleeves" they simply cut off your hands.

Tree's telephone rang. He peered at the number on the display and didn't recognize it. He'd had enough unexpected trouble for one day. But then he was a detective, wasn't he? He was supposed to be a tough guy, or at least tough enough to pick up a telephone.

"Trembath here," said the voice on the other end of the line.

"Mr. Trembath," Tree said.

"Any news, old chap?"

"I was hoping you might be calling with some," Tree said.

"No news from this end, I'm afraid. Mr. Shah has left the island for a few days. But he's anxious to be kept in touch about any developments."

"What do you know about a man named Edgar Bunya?"

There was an interesting silence before Trembath said: "I don't know anyone by that name."

"How about Javor Zoran?"

Another silence. "Why am I supposed to know these people?"

"Their names have come up during the course of my investigation," Tree said.

"Mr. Shah is not interested in anything but results—quick results. I do hope you're not going to let him down."

"I wouldn't dream of it," Tree said. "I'm off to Key West tomorrow."

"Key West?" Trembath sounded unexpectedly irritated. "Why would you go to Key West?"

"Let's just say I'm playing out a lead."

"I do hope you're not wasting your time, Mr. Callister. I don't know why Mrs. Traven would be in Key West."

"Then where do you suggest I look for her?"

That produced yet another pause. "Well, that's what we hired you for, isn't it?"

"Then let me go to Key West."

"Yes, of course, I'm not going to bloody well stop you, am I?" A forced jocularity was back in his voice. "Well, Mr. Callister, good luck and cheers."

Trembath hung up his phone.

# 10

I met Hemingway once in Rome," Rex Baxter was saying, leaning against the bar at the Lighthouse.

As usual on a Fun Friday, Rex was surrounded by an array of tourist-acolytes who remembered him from his Chicago television days.

"He came in to Harry's Bar on the Via Veneto and then Sinatra came in and there we were standing around shooting the breeze. Frank was waiting for Ava but she never showed up that night."

Someone said in an awed voice, "You were drinking with Hemingway *and* Sinatra?"

"Well, that was Rome in those days," Rex said. "Everybody was there, and if you were there, you were at Harry's. Anyway, Hemingway was Papa by then, the legend, the great white hunter with the beard and the safari jacket, the whole bit. We got to talking about movies, him and me and Sinatra. Hemingway *hated* Hollywood. Oh, he took their money all right, but he hated what they did to his books, and wouldn't have anything to do with writing scripts. I admired him for that. Everyone else, Fitzgerald, Faulkner,

Raymond Chandler, they all sold out to Hollywood. Whatever you might think of Hemingway, he never sold out. He remained true to himself."

The rest of what Rex said was drowned out by the electronic piano player's version of "Mandy." Tree turned and leaned into Freddie's ear and said, "Not that you're keeping track but the count is up to three for the people looking for Elizabeth."

"Who's trying to find her?"

"There's the Pakistani spy I told you about, Miram Shan."

"Okay. Who else?"

"Javor Zoran. He's a big Serb who wears flip-flops and doesn't cut his toenails. He also tries to sound dangerous."

"Tries?"

"You don't take him too seriously until you find out that the War Crimes Tribunal in The Hague was going to indict him, but then had second thoughts."

"About what?"

"The number of people he murdered. Apparently, he didn't kill enough people for it to qualify as a crime against humanity."

"You meet the nicest people, Tree."

"And let's not forget Dr. Edgar Bunya, the latest addition to the growing list of Elizabeth's admirers."

"Who is this guy?"

"I'm not so sure about him. From what I can figure, he may be some sort of rebel from Sierra Leone. Dr. Bunya owns a machete."

"What's he doing with a machete?"

"Actually, the correct term, according to him, is cutlass. He says he's going to use it to give me short sleeves unless I tell him where Elizabeth is."

"What's this about short sleeves?"

"That is Sierra Leone rebel speak for cutting off your hands."

"Good grief, Tree."

"That's why I had better find Elizabeth."

"But you don't know where she is."

"Zoran thinks she might be in Key West. I'm going to check it out tomorrow."

"I don't think you should go to Key West."

"I know."

"'I know,' as in 'You're right, honey. I'm not going.' Or 'I know' as in, 'I'm going, anyway, and to heck with what you think?'"

"I'm being driven by Miram Shah's money, not to mention Javor Zoran's. And I've got visions of Dr. Edgar Bunya's cutlass, and what happens if I don't find her."

"Do I have to tell you to be careful?"

"Careful is my middle name."

"No, it isn't, but you're past the point where I can talk any sense into you." He couldn't tell whether she was angry, suspected she was. She looked at her watch. "I've got to get out of here. I'm to meet my people in a few minutes."

"Your syndicate that's going to buy Dayton's," Tree said.

"Investors. They've flown in from Milwaukee and Chicago," she said.

"I didn't even know you knew anyone in Milwaukee."

"I know someone in Tulsa too, but he couldn't make it."

"So this looks like it's going to happen."

"Nothing's happening yet," Freddie cautioned. "It's just a get-acquainted meeting."

"I'm amazed it's moved this quickly."

Freddie put her hand on his arm. "Are you all right with this?"

"Of course," Tree said. "Why wouldn't I be?"

"You have to admit this whole situation is a little weird."

"Listen," Tree said, "life in general is weird these days. I'm encountering doctors armed with machetes. Buying supermarkets is nothing. If this is what you want, I'm all for it."

"Thank you, my love." She leaned forward and gently kissed him. Then she looked at her watch again and said, "Are you going to stay?"

"For a few minutes. Chris said he might show up. I'll meet you back at the house."

"If I'm going to be late, I'll call you." She gave him another peck on the mouth before making her exit.

The music stopped. Rex was saying, "Hollywood always messed Hemingway up, maybe that's why he hated the town. I mean look at what Darryl Zanuck did to the 20th Century Fox version of *The Sun Also Rises*.

"The novel is about a lost generation of young people in Paris in the 1920s. So who does Zanuck get for the movie? Tyrone Power and Errol Flynn, who were both in their forties. Even Ava Gardner was too old for Lady Brett Ashley. What was Zanuck thinking? But that was the town in the 1950s. They always cast everything too old because there were all these ancient stars hanging around. So young actresses like Grace Kelly and Audrey Hepburn played against guys old enough to be their fathers.

"I mean, when Grace married Gary Cooper in *High Noon*, he looked like her *grandfather*. But Coop was good in *For Whom The Bell Tolls*, although I don't think Hemingway liked that, either. He liked Coop, though. He and Coop were pals. *The Killers* with Burt Lancaster and Ava Gardner was the best of Hemingway's stuff on the screen. Hemingway even had a copy of it, which he liked to watch when he was at his place in Cuba."

Tree enjoyed listening to Rex. He'd been hearing the stories for a lifetime. Neither Rex nor his stories had changed much; they had just found a more receptive home on Sanibel. In Chicago, Rex had been a failed actor and minor local TV personality. Here on Sanibel Island he was royalty, coddled and courted, surrounded by adoring tourists who loved his memories of another time and all the famous people who inhabited that time. If the two of them were to end their days here, then Rex would end them happily. Tree was not so certain about himself.

"Dad?"

Tree turned to find Chris standing there, the light from the bar glinting off his glasses. He had a big, happy smile on his face and his arm around a young woman.

"Dad," he said, "I'd like you to meet my friend, Susan."

Tree looked into the fiercely blue eyes of Cailie Fisk.

# 11

Susan?" Tree had trouble getting the word out of his mouth.

She smiled and said, "Susan Troy," holding out a slim hand to him. He took it, feeling the electric warmth of her touch. The blue eyes revealed nothing.

"We thought we'd drop around and say hello," he heard Chris say. "We're just on our way to dinner."

Tree stared at the two of them. Chris said, "Where's Freddie?"

Tree rallied and said, "She had a meeting. You just missed her."

"I'm so sorry," Susan said. "Chris has been raving about her."

Chris said, "Would you like something to drink, Susan?"

"A kir royale," she said.

Chris grinned. "Kir royale? Wasn't that your drink of choice in Paris in the old days, Dad?"

"Cassis with champagne." Susan's eyes were on Tree. "I learned to drink it in Paris, too."

Chris turned to Matt the bartender and asked if he could make a kir royale. He nodded. "One part cassis to five parts champagne. I pour the cassis into a flute and then add the champagne."

"Make one for me, please," Susan said.

Matt said, "Coming up." He soon returned with a champagne glass filled with pale red liquid. Tree presented it to Susan. "There you go," he said.

"It always makes me think of Paris," Susan said, aiming an appreciative smile at Tree. "What about you?"

"What about me?"

"Does it make you think of Paris, Mr. Callister?"

"Please, call me Tree."

"It was named after a guy who was the mayor of Lyon in the 1940s," Rex said, wandering over. Chris introduced Susan. "Rex is the president of the Chamber of Commerce here on Sanibel," Chris explained. "He and Dad have been friends forever."

"Only since dinosaurs ruled the earth," Rex said. "I found Tree in the forest and raised him as my own."

"Rex used to be an actor in Hollywood," Chris said.

"Hollywood." Susan sounded impressed. "Were you in anything I might have seen?"

"I was Jack Palance's young pal in *I Died A Thousand Times*," Rex said.

Cailie shifted her attention back to Tree. "Chris says you're a detective."

"Only detective on Sanibel," Rex said. "He's a tourist attraction."

"Dangerous work?"

"Not really," Tree said.

"Don't let my father fool you," Chris said. "He's had his share of trouble."

"You look like a man who could get himself into trouble, all right," she said.

"Where are you from Susan?" Tree asked.

She put her glass on the bar and turned to Chris. "We'll be late for dinner."

Chris finished his wine and said, "Okay, let's get going."

Cailie blessed Tree with yet another direct blue-eyed gaze. "Pleasure to meet you, Mr. Callister."

"Tree."

"Tree."

You never answered my question."

"What was that, Tree?"

"Where you are from."

"Just outside St. Louis." She took Chris's arm. "All set?"

"See you later," Chris said, and off they went.

Rex looked Tree up and down. "What was that all about?"

"What was what all about?"

"You and that woman. She looked at you like she knew you."

"You're imagining things."

"Hey, you're talking to me, kemo sabe."

Tree shrugged. "Chris mentioned the other day he'd met someone. Maybe I'm a little concerned that this may not be the right time to be chasing blondes around Sanibel Island, that's all."

"Because the cops still have their eye on him for the Kendra Callister murder."

Now it was Tree's turn to stare at Rex. "What have you heard?"

"Just that. The view is that maybe Ray Dayton killed Kendra, but maybe he didn't. Sure they found Ray's sperm in her. But they also found Chris's."

Tree put what was left of his water on the bar. "I'm going to get out of here," he said.

"Sorry if I upset you," Rex said.

"No, it's all right. Nothing to do with you, Rex. Fun Friday isn't much fun tonight, that's all."

---

Freddie still wasn't home when he got back to Andy Rosse Lane. That gave him time to consider his shock at finding Chris with Cailie Fisk or Susan Troy or whatever her name was. He reminded himself again that nothing had happened between them. There was no scandal here. Okay, but then why hadn't he told Freddie that? Perhaps because something *had* happened. No matter how much he tried to rationalize it, he had ended up in a young woman's hotel room late at night in Paris. He could claim innocence all he wanted, but it didn't *appear* innocent. Even if Freddie said she believed him, there would still be a shadow lingering over their marriage that had never been there before.

Someone was ringing the front door bell. Who would be calling at this time of night? He went to the door and opened it to find Vera Dayton swaying on the doorstep.

"Vera," he said.

"Freddie," Vera said. "I want to talk to Freddie."

"She's not here right now," Tree said.

Vera barged past him. He caught the whiff of scotch and realized she was drunk. In the living room, Vera flopped on a sofa, a small, stout woman, the remnants of blond youth still visible in the round smoothness of her face. Tonight, however, her eyes were cloudy and unfocused and her lip kept curling in a way that lent her unintended meanness—or maybe not so unintended.

"I've come to tell Freddie I'm not going to let her do it," she said in a slurred voice. "It's not gonna happen."

"Did you drive over here, Vera?" Tree kept his voice steady, trying to avoid doing anything that would spark a confrontation with Ray Dayton's inebriated widow.

"I didn't want Ray to hire her, you know," Vera went on. "I told him not to do it. She wasn't needed. Wasn't wanted. But as usual, he didn't listen to me, and now he's dead, and the last thing I want is her taking over."

"Now is probably not the time to be talking about this, Vera."

Her head shot up, momentarily lifting the clouds from her eyes. "He loved her, you know." Vera making a formal accusation. "He was crazy about Freddie."

"I know all about it," Tree said.

She issued a drunken smirk. "You *think* you know, Mr. Tree Callister. But you don't know it all. You don't know everything."

"What don't I know, Vera?"

"You don't have a cigarette, do you?"

"Sorry, Vera," Tree said, wondering how the devil he was going to get her out of here.

"That's right. Tree Callister doesn't smoke. He doesn't drink. He's a good boy, that Tree Callister." She issued a snort of laughter. "But we know, Tree. We know. Don't we?"

Tree just stared at her, certain that anything he said would only further antagonize her.

She gave another snort of laughter. "There are things I could tell you, Mr. Sunset Detective. You think you're smart, but you're not smart at all."

She put her head back against the sofa, and the next thing Tree knew she was snoring gently.

That's how Freddie found her when she came in a few minutes later. "When did she get here?"

"Not long ago," Tree said. "She says she doesn't want you taking over her business."

"That's what she said?"

"A number of times. But she's pretty loaded."

"Well, we can't let her drive home."

Freddie gently shook her. Vera smacked her lips loudly and sat up. When she saw Freddie she put on a bleary smile. "I'm drunk, Freddie. Sorry."

"We're going to drive you home," Freddie said.

"No, I can drive all right," Vera said.

Freddie helped her to her feet. "It's no problem. Tree and I have to go out, anyway. We'll just drop you off. It's better that way."

"You're not a bad person, Freddie. You're really not."

"Let's go out to the car, Vera."

"This is kind of you," Vera said. "But I can drive. Really, I can." Vera collapsed against Freddie who caught her and made sure she didn't fall to the floor.

With Tree's help, they got her outside. Vera's Jaguar was on the lawn. She had left the driver's side door open. Tree closed it and then helped Freddie put Vera into the back seat of the Mercedes.

Freddie got behind the wheel and then Tree went to the Jag and climbed in. The key was still in the ignition. He started the motor, and the Jag rumbled contentedly as he backed it onto the roadway.

Tree followed Freddie's tail lights to Vera and Ray's rambling one-story house at the Sanctuary, the island's only gated community. Tree parked the Jag in the drive and watched as Freddie escorted a woozy-but-conscious Vera inside the house. Ten minutes later she was back.

"I'm sorry about that," Freddie said.

"I don't think she's ever gotten over the fact her husband was in love with you," Tree said.

"Ray wasn't in love with me," Freddie said.

"That's what Vera thinks."

"Whatever it was, it wasn't love."

---

Later, when they were in bed, Tree, unable to sleep, twisted around, trying to block out the lion's roar.

*The lion's roar?*

He sat up on the camp cot, hearing it again. He got up and pushed back the canvas tent flap and stepped into a clearing lit by the glow of a camp fire. He was surprised to see Freddie seated by the fire close to a muscular, black-haired fellow with the rather cruelly-handsome face of a young Sean Connery. The two of them glanced up quickly as he approached—rather guiltily, Tree thought.

"Did you hear the sound of that lion?" Tree said.

"Let's not talk about the lion," Freddie said.

"Why not?" said Tree. "Why can't we talk about the lion?"

"It's a damn fine lion," said the Sean Connery guy. "What'll it be, Macomber? Shall I have the mess boy make you a gimlet?"

"Macomber?" said Tree. "You mean Francis Macomber?"

"You're a coward," Freddie said, poking at the fire with a stick, making quick, angry thrusts. "That's why I slept with him."

"Who? Who did you sleep with?" Tree demanded.

"Wilson here. The white hunter. After you ran from the lion. After you showed yourself to be a coward, I thought it was time I was with a real man."

"You're not supposed to say that," Tree protested. "I'm supposed to read it between the lines. The way Hemingway would have had it."

"It's a damn fine lion," Wilson said.

"To hell with between the lines," Freddie said. "I slept with him. You might as well know it. You've always been a coward. You've always tried to conceal it, first in the newspaper business and then by becoming a detective. You did everything you could to hide your fear. But now you've confronted the lion and run away, and everyone knows the truth about you."

The white hunter grinned and said, "Sure you won't have a gimlet?"

"A what?" Tree said.

"A gimlet," Freddie said. "Do you want a gimlet?"

"I don't want a gimlet."

"Only cowards refuse to drink gimlets," Freddie said. "They don't drink and they run away from the lion."

"I didn't run," Tree protested. "I didn't. I'm not a coward."

The white hunter grinned sardonically. "It's a damn fine lion. Sure you don't want a gimlet?"

"Tree. Tree, wake up."

He opened his eyes. Freddie, still in her pajamas, was standing over him. "It's six o'clock," she said.

"I don't want a gimlet," he said.

"What?" she said.

He got up from their bed. There was no sign of a campfire or a white hunter who looked like Sean Connery.

"You'd better hurry or you're going to miss the boat to Key West," Freddie said.

"Yes," he said.

"And what's all this stuff about a gimlet?"

# 12

Just before dawn, Tree drove into the parking lot adjacent to the Key West Express dock. He locked the Beetle and then walked over to the ramp leading to the ticket office where other passengers were already lined up, tourists mostly, somber and still half asleep.

Tree showed his photo identification—a requirement before they would let you on the boat—and paid for his ticket. He crossed to where the giant catamaran—"the Big Cat"—was docked, went aboard, got himself a coffee, and then found a seat on the upper level. The boat quickly filled with passengers. Presently, the diesel engines started up, members of the crew cast off the lines at either end of the vessel, and the catamaran moved away from the dock, churning out the harbor, past Fort Myers Beach condos lined up like white dominos along the shore.

Tree leaned against a railing as the Key West Express passed beneath the San Carlos Bridge. A sailboat swooped past, shining in the morning sun, inspiring a flurry of excited waving from Tree's fellow passengers.

Tree found a seat out of the already hot sun. Not far away, three large men roared with laughter, enjoying their first beers of the day. The ferry finally cleared the harbor and the jet-propelled diesels went into action as the craft made an arcing left, picking up speed, Fort Myers Beach fading behind the wake's creamy foam.

For the first hour or so the sea remained calm, the sky clear, and Tree enjoyed the ride. He tried not to think of Elizabeth Traven or Susan Troy, née Cailie Fisk, or the half-truths he had told Freddie. He finished his coffee and then climbed the stairs to the upper deck for a better view of the sea. He inhaled the salty air, waving to the passing tourist boats and pleasure craft.

At mid-morning clouds blotted the sun, darkening the sky. The wind rose and the sea grew choppy. The coffee sloshed around in Tree's stomach. He didn't feel well. He went back down to his mid-decks seat. That didn't help. He felt queasier than ever. The Big Cat shook every time it hit a high wave.

Finally, Tree retreated below decks to one of the air-line-type easy chairs in the main lounge. He broke into a sweat as his stomach roiled violently. He stared at the floor, trying not to think about throwing up. He twisted around to identify the location of rest rooms, groaning, thinking about how much he hated water and boats; the madness of living in a tropical world defined by both.

"Here, take this." A hand held out a plastic bag. "You can throw up in it."

He took the bag as Cailie Fisk slipped into the seat beside him. He had a moment to observe her form-fitting blouse and jeans before he lowered his head into the bag and brought up the coffee and whatever else churned in his betraying stomach.

Cailie put her hand on his shoulder as his stomach twisted again, and his body shuddered, ejecting more liquid into the bag.

When it was over she said, "Here, let me take that." She plucked the bag from his fingers and was gone. Great, he thought as he gasped for air. The last person in the world he wanted to throw up in front of, and not only was he doing just that, but she was helping him.

She returned, handing him a couple of tissues. He pressed them against his perspiring face. His stomach began to settle.

He said, "What are you doing?"

"I'm trying to help you."

"What are you doing here?"

"What do you think? I'm going to Key West."

"You're following me."

She snorted with laughter. "That's rather arrogant, don't you think?"

He sat back, taking deep breaths. Around him, he could hear passenger voices over the throb of the jet engines. Voices that appeared to be enjoying the ride. He glanced around. No one else was puking into plastic bags. He felt foolish and embarrassed.

"Come on. Susan or Cailie or whatever your name is, you manage to insinuate yourself into my life in Paris—"

"Is that what happened?" She laughed. "I *insinuated* myself into your life?"

"And the next thing you're on the island. I approach you at the Visitors Center and you deny you even know me. Then you reappear with my son at the Lighthouse."

She stood and smiled down at him. "You think too much of yourself, Tree."

"Why did you tell my son your name is Susan Troy?"

"Maybe that's my name," she said.

"Then why did you tell me it's Cailie Fisk?"

"I hope you're feeling better."

When she went to move away, he grabbed her wrist and that wiped away the smile. "Don't do that," she said sharply.

"That's how you knew I was in Paris, wasn't it? Chris told you. You followed us there. But why?"

Her face had gone flat. "Let go of my wrist," she said. He released her. "Why? Why are you doing this?"

"Maybe I've decided to move to Sanibel. Maybe I've decided that you're not much of a detective, and there might be room for another detective on the island."

He stared up at her. "You're kidding."

The smile had returned, brighter than ever. "Someone who can get things done, who doesn't hide things, who can solve unsolved murders. I think I would be good at that."

She swayed off along the aisle. Several male heads swiveled to watch her appreciatively.

Tree sat with unfocused eyes on one of the LCD screens in front of him. Two heavyset sports commentators, bursting out of shiny suits, silently opened and closed their mouths. They were talking about football he didn't understand, on a boat he hated, in a state surrounded on three sides by water that made him sick. What was he doing here, bedeviled by a weak stomach and threatening women?

# 13

Tree stood, taking deep, gulping breaths of air. By now the boat had slowed, entering calmer waters as it approached Key West. He made his way up on the deck and was immediately hit by a wave of warm air and a gentle sea breeze that helped clear his head. He stood at the railing, and watched the tiny figures hovering above him, suspended in the blue Key West sky harnessed to brightly colored parachutes. Beachfront homes with screened-in porches were scattered among palm trees. Ahead on the left, a coastguard vessel lay like a roughly hewn piece of ivory at dockside.

He came down the gangplank after the Key West Express docked and made his way along a covered walkway looking for Susan or Cailie or whatever the blazes her name was. There was no sign of her. Why? He asked himself for the hundredth time. Why all the dishonesty, the elaborate deceits? What was the point? Because he refused to sleep with her in Paris? He was a sixty-year-old man. She was a beauty in her thirties. Even in his wildest fit of arrogant narcissism—and there had been enough of those over the years—he could not imagine his animal appeal lay behind her decision to come to Sanibel.

When he couldn't find a taxi, a pedicab driver named Marco insisted Tree should ride with him. "Can you take me to the Southernmost House?" Tree asked.

"No problem," Marco said.

Tree climbed into the cab while Marco clambered onto the bicycle, announcing he would take a route that avoided the crowds along Duval. Tree said that was fine.

Marco started off, moving along artfully shaded residential streets lined with the traditional conch houses originally built by salvage wreckers and sponge fishermen from the Bahamas who had brought with them Florida's most unique architecture.

Marco said he was from Serbia, working in Key West on a student visa. The local economy could not get along without guys like him, he said.

Tree telephoned Freddie. To his surprise she picked up immediately. "I'm calling you from a Key West pedicab," Tree said.

"So you are okay?"

"If you don't count the fact that I threw up on the boat," he said.

"You are not a man of the sea," she said.

"We will not be sailing around the world," Tree agreed. "Is Elizabeth at the hotel?"

"I haven't checked yet."

"What are you going to do if she isn't?"

To avoid answering that question, he said, "I wish you were here. This pedicab would be a lot more fun with you in it."

"You haven't answered my question. What are you going to do?"

"I'm not quite sure," he said.

"Sounds like this is a bit of a wild goose chase."

"I'm going to find her," Tree insisted.

"I believe you," Freddie said.

"You don't sound very convinced."

"Listen, I've got to go. They're holding a meeting for me. We're about to sit down with Vera. Wish me luck."

"Good luck," Tree said.

"Call me tonight," she said. "Let me know you're all right."

The Southernmost House, in its brightly painted turn-of-the-century glory, stood at the corner of Duval and South Streets. Tree paid off Marco, wished him luck, and walked through the gate into the hotel's courtyard.

The Persian carpet in the Southernmost lobby matched the dark wood fireplace and the dark wood desk where a smiling young man said to a middle-aged couple, "The house was a speakeasy in the 1920s, during prohibition."

"Was that legal?" asked the woman.

The young man—Kevin according to his name tag—smiled indulgently. "This was Key West, of course. So what was legal or illegal was always up for grabs. Mr. Al Capone himself was a guest. Someone took a shot at him right here in the lobby."

"I wonder what room he stayed in?" said the man.

"We're not sure about that," Kevin said. "But Mr. Al Capone was here, that's for sure. The man himself."

Kevin fixed the tourists with a town map, issued directions to the Hemingway house on Whitehead Street, and ordered them to have "a great day," before turning his attention to Tree. "Welcome to the Southernmost House, sir. How may I help you?"

Tree said, "I believe a friend of mine is staying here. A woman named Elizabeth Traven. Can you tell me what room she's in?"

Kevin's frown returned. "That name doesn't ring a bell, but let me check." He went to work on the computer keyboard. Even before his fingers had stopped moving, he was shaking his head. "No, Mr. Callister. I'm afraid no one by that name has checked in recently. Also, we don't have a reservation under that name."

"Okay, thanks," Tree said.

So much for quickly finding Elizabeth and putting an end to this, he thought. Now what was he supposed to do? If she wasn't at the hotel, where was she? Maybe not even in Key West. The thought depressed him.

Then he remembered the photo of Elizabeth with Javor Zoran. As soon as he saw it, Kevin's face lit with recognition. "She was here last week, but not under that name."

"But she's not here now?"

"No, she checked out a few days ago," Kevin said. "I remember because she was with Mr. Hank Dearlove."

"Who's Hank Dearlove?" Tree asked.

"He's one of our local guides at the Hemingway Estate," Kevin said.

# 14

The fine old Spanish colonial house where Ernest Hemingway had resided in Key West was at 907 Whitehead Street.

Tree paid the entrance fee at the ticket booth. A white-bearded man wearing a baseball cap who could have been Hemingway's brother stood at the main entrance doors. "There's a guided tour in fifteen minutes," he said.

"I'm looking for Hank Dearlove," Tree said.

"Hank's conducting the tour," the white-bearded man said,

Inside the entry hall, more old guys with white beards wearing baseball caps nodded at Tree and directed him into a sitting room where a group of about twenty was already gathered. Tree inspected a salmon-colored settee, trying to imagine Hemingway sitting on it.

A voice behind him said, "Everyone, listen up, please. I am Hank, and this afternoon I will be your guide into the life and times of one Ernest Hemingway, author, and Key West resident."

Tree turned to see a tall, aristocratic man in his sixties, pale, with blondish-white hair thrown carelessly back from a high forehead. He wore khaki trousers, sandals, and a flowered shirt that did not hang loosely enough to hide an unexpectedly generous belly.

Hank Dearlove raised his arms as though addressing the heavens. "Hemingway!" He paused for effect. "That name stirs passions and contradictions. For some, and I include myself in this group, the name conjures visions of masculinity, romance, and courage of a sort we don't much recognize any more. Maybe that's what keeps bringing many of us back to him. Maybe we want the big game hunter, the deep-sea fisherman, the passionate writer in the Paris of the 1920s, the warrior, the journalist. We want this guy. But who is it we want? How do we put flesh and blood onto the mythology of our greatest American writer?"

Hank lowered his arms and smiled. "Well, I'm not so sure how much flesh and blood we can provide Mr. Hemingway today or whether it's even possible. No other American writer has been as inspected and speculated about, related and deflated as old Ernie. Yet I'm not so sure we know any more about him today than we did when he died in 1961. But at least in this house this afternoon, good friends, I can show you where he lived and worked. You are within the walls where he existed. Perhaps you will be able to feel his presence. He was here. In many ways, perhaps, he is still here. He haunts these walls. He haunts us all."

Abruptly Hank wheeled out of the room. "Follow me," he called.

Everyone obediently filed across the hall into the dining room where Hank briefly sketched Hemingway's early life, including his childhood in Oak Park, Illinois; the mother who dressed him in little girl's clothes (although not much was made of that); the father who committed suicide; the young man wounded in the Spanish civil war; the journalist sent by the *Toronto Star* to Paris in the twenties; his first wife, Hadley; her best friend, Pauline Pfeiffer.

"Lust in Paris," Hank declared. "Youthful Mr. Hemingway appeared incapable of simply sleeping with a woman; he had to marry her. So he dumped Hadley and married Pauline, who fulfilled the other requirement Mr. Hemingway had of his women: money. Ernest didn't have any; his wives did.

"It was Pauline's uncle who bought this house for them," Hank continued. "A generous uncle, no? Even in 1931, this was an expensive home—the finest in Key West. Pauline brought the chandeliers you see here, and the decorative taste, which may or may not be to your liking. Not to mine, but then I would not have so easily dumped Hadley, the most attractive of Mr. Hemingway's women, not counting Miss Ava Gardner, of course. He was infatuated with Miss Ava, but I have my doubts whether he ever slept with her."

As he talked, Hank moved to a portrait of a dark-haired, mustached Hemingway, surprisingly handsome. "Now, of course, the prevailing image of Mr. Hemingway is that of the white-bearded old hunter. 'Papa' Hemingway. The famous Karsh portrait; the prototype for all aging writers, including many of the guides you will see wandering around here today.

"But that is not the Hemingway who inhabits this place." His arm swept up in the direction of the painting. "*This* is the Hemingway who lived in Key West. Young, virile, full of the juices of life. You study this portrait, and you understand how this youthful stud took the literary world by storm. A superstar, imbued with that rough masculinity, very much of its time. The same sort of manliness that made Gable and Cooper and Tracy movie stars. No Justins back then, Bieber or Timberlake. These were *men*. They went to war, and drank hard, and shot wild animals, and fished in the sea, and slept with any woman they could get their hands on, preferably a beauty. All gone today—more's the pity."

A few women present murmured objection. Hank's eyebrows shot up in feigned surprise. "Oh, my, have I offended some here? Well, I suppose I have, but it's a minor offense. Remember, please, you are in Mr. Hemingway's country for the moment, the thinking is old-fashioned and very different. Perhaps I'm merely giving you a taste of it; no more than that."

Hank quelled further dissent by herding his charges up narrow stairs to the second floor master bedroom. A ginger cat curled on the bed where once, according to Hank, Hemingway and Pauline had slept and loved. "Now, alas, only cats inhabit that connubial bed." Hank in wistful voice.

He brightened as he swept a hand over the sleeping ginger cat: "Behold one of our famous Hemingway cats. These are the direct descendants of the felines nurtured by Ernest and Pauline while they lived here. The more formal name for this cat is a polydactyl—a feline with a genetic mutation that results in being born with more than the usual number of toes on at least one of its paws. This fellow, as you can see, has six toes on his front left paw."

Several visitors duly petted and stroked the cat which stretched luxuriously, purring loudly, enjoying the attention.

Finally, Hank led his merry band of Hemingway followers out to the pool house. "There on the second floor Mr. Hemingway wrote *To Have and Have Not*." Another dramatic pause. "The worst piece of crap Mr. Hemingway ever produced, in my estimation."

This caused nervous titters and small gasps of astonishment. "Don't be so shocked. Mr. Hemingway could write bad books just like anyone else. He was not a god, after all. He was a real man and real men fail from time to time. But men are also capable of greatness, and one only has to read *The Sun Also Rises* to know Mr. Hemingway achieved that greatness."

Hank then chose Tree and three others to make the climb up wrought iron stairs to peer through an iron latticework divider into a wide, bright room. An antelope head adorned the wall over a portable typewriter on a round table.

"A walkway used to connect the master bedroom to the office," Hank explained. "That way, he merely had to get out of bed in the morning, cross over to the office, and go to work."

"What do you think, Mr. Dearlove?" Tree squeezed himself in beside Hank. "What happened in there to make *To Have and Have Not* such a lousy novel?"

Dearlove looked momentarily surprised at being addressed by his surname. Then he said, "Maybe it was his lousy marriage. He was too distracted, just didn't give a damn."

The other three tourists began to file back down the stairs. Hank called for four more to come up. He turned back to Tree. "Seen enough?"

"I think we should talk," Tree said.

"About Hemingway?"

"About Elizabeth Traven," Tree said.

"And who might wish to discuss such a subject?"

"I'm Tree Callister. I'm a private detective."

"Are you now?" Hank did not appear impressed.

"I'm here looking for her."

"Well, she's not at the Hemingway Estate, I can tell you that much. I don't think Elizabeth even likes Hemingway." He showed a neat row of yellowing teeth. "Why don't you go back downstairs, Mr. Tree Callister, have a look in the gift shop. Maybe you'd like a Hemingway T-shirt. As soon as I'm finished here, I'll find you."

---

Tree spent some time poking around the gift shop. When he came out, he found Hank on a bench near the pool talking to a lingering elderly couple.

"So Hemingway gets home from Spain, where he'd been having it off with Martha Gelhorn," Hank said. "Pauline, meanwhile, got wind of the affair and as revenge spent twenty thousand dollars building this swimming pool. The entire house only cost eight thousand. Ernest was furious. 'You've cost me everything,' he yelled at her. 'Here, you might as well have my last red cent.' And he threw a penny down on the ground. Pauline, who I guess had a sense of humor, had it embedded in the cement."

He pointed a finger at a coin implanted in one of the deck stones. "And there it is."

The couple chuckled nervously, uncertain whether Hemingway the adulterer was amusing. The husband slipped Hank a ten-dollar bill. His wife thanked him for the entertaining and informative tour, albeit a little controversial.

The elderly couple drifted off, and Tree joined Hank on the bench. The late afternoon sun threw long shadows across Hemingway's lushly tropical backyard.

"You didn't buy a T-shirt."

"No."

"Funny. You struck me as the kind of guy who might wear a Hemingway T-shirt."

"That's not a compliment, is it?"

"No, it isn't." Hank grinned.

"Anything to that last red cent story?"

Hank shrugged. "As true as anything, I suppose. Is the furniture in the house his?" Another shrug. "Well, Mr. Hemingway and Pauline divorced in 1940. She kept the house, since she paid for it, and lived here until she died in 1951. She and Hadley rekindled their friendship, incidentally. I suppose they had a lot to talk about.

"After Pauline was gone, the house reverted back to Mr. Hemingway, but he never returned. The place was sold to a local businesswoman in 1961. She held onto it until there were so many tourists pounding on the door it was decided to turn it into a museum. Hard to believe the original furniture survived all that. Nevertheless, we tell them it's real. For all I know it is. And for all I know, Mr. Callister, you are a harmless enough individual who might be tempted to buy a T-shirt in Key West, but who otherwise should steer clear of the trouble you seem bound and determined to get into."

"Are you in love with Elizabeth Traven?"

He seemed slightly taken aback by the question. "Should I be?"

"Everyone else seems to be."

"Elizabeth is the sort of woman you watch carefully, Mr. Callister. You don't fall in love with her—that is if you've got any brains."

"Where Elizabeth is concerned, men don't seem to have them."

"You could be talking about yourself, Mr. Callister."

"Is she still in Key West?"

"Mr. Callister, you are a private detective, is that correct?"

"Yes," Tree said.

"I'm afraid you have been sent here by idiots to do an idiot's work."

"What about you, Dearlove? You appear to be mixed up with them."

"If I was, I soon realized I had made a mistake. You would be wise to do the same thing."

"And do what?"

"Buy your T-shirt at the gift shop, and then go away and forget about all this."

"Answer my question first. Is Elizabeth in Key West?"

"I have no idea where she is."

"Suppose I think you're lying."

The watery smile was back as Hank heaved himself to his feet. "The people who hired you are old fools, involved in something they should never have become involved in. Meaning no disrespect to you, Mr. Callister, stumbling amateurs have hired an amateur to work for them. Your enthusiasm is commendable, but if you push this any further, you are going to get into a lot of trouble, and it will end badly for you, I promise."

"Everyone I meet threatens me these days."

"Some threats you should take more seriously than others," Hank said.

"Yours, for instance?"

"You might be wise."

If you see Elizabeth, tell her I'd like to talk to her."

"Mention my name at the gift shop," Hank said. "You'll get a twenty-five per cent discount on that T-shirt."

Hank moved off, displaying a certain frayed elegance even in sandals. Tree studied Hemingway's penny embedded in the pool deck.

# 15

Tree Callister, intrepid private eye, stood outside the Hemingway Estate, trying to think what to do next. Hank Dearlove had not turned out to be much help. Tree was uncertain whether Elizabeth was even in Key West. Dearlove had suggested that since Tree had been hired by fools, he was probably a fool himself.

Standing there, trying to think of the next move, Tree couldn't disagree.

Dusk was falling now. The gates had closed. Whitehead Street was empty except for the Range Rover. Tree hadn't noticed it before. It was parked at the curb, a few yards away.

Suddenly, the Rover leapt forward and screeched to a stop so close it made him jump back in alarm. Two big Latino men leaped out. One wore a pork pie hat while the other was in a broad-brimmed straw hat. Pork Pie Hat grabbed Tree and threw him against the vehicle. Immediately, the second Latino in the straw hat was pressing something into his back, hissing in his ear: "Get in, hombre, and don't argue about it."

Tree allowed himself to be propelled forward into the Rover's interior.

"Get over there," Straw Hat ordered.

Tree scrambled awkwardly across the seat while Straw Hat crowded in beside him. Pork Pie Hat was in the front behind the wheel.

"What is this?" demanded Tree.

"What is this?" said Pork Pie Hat. "Right now this is nothing. This is a drive. Give us any trouble and it's a whole lot of something else. So sit quiet and enjoy the ride."

Straw Hat beside him now had a gun that he held up so Tree could see it. When he smiled, he had a couple of front teeth missing.

The toothless gunman said, "Don't worry about doing up your seatbelt, hombre."

---

Conch house-lined residential streets flashed past as the Range Rover turned left and then right, and then executed a bewildering series of left-right turns. The driver kept hitting the brakes and jerking the vehicle to hard stops before gunning it again—erratic enough to make Tree's stomach spin.

Great, he thought. The tough guy private detective would frighten his captors by throwing up on them. Is this how Hemingway would have acted had a couple of toughs grabbed him outside his house? Doubtful. Visions of Francis Macomber confronting the lion flashed through his mind—Macomber cowering in the back seat of a Range Rover.

The driver clamped on the brakes one last time and the Range Rover shuddered to a stop. The straw hat with the gun ordered him out.

Tree opened the side door and slid out into uncertain darkness. Fish smells carried on sea air assailed his nostrils. Tree Callister, the Sherlock Holmes of Florida detectives, concluded he had been deposited somewhere near the waterfront which, in Key West, could be just about anywhere.

A light snapped on, throwing an amber glow over a long table pushed against a cinderblock wall. A pink box wrapped in a red ribbon lay on the table beside a machete.

Edgar Bunya stepped into the circle of light. Tree's stomach tightened. Edgar once again was in a beautifully tailored, pinstriped suit, his high-collared, snow-white shirt offset by a bright blue tie. He was not wearing a hat, but he carried a lily. He smiled when he saw Tree, and he said, "My friend."

He laid the lily on the table beside the machete and the pink box.

"Ganache," he said.

"The filling in the macaron," Tree said. "You didn't know what it was."

"I have since done some investigating," Edgar said. "It's a glaze or sauce made of cream and dark chocolate."

"You don't say," Tree said, trying to keep the strain out of his voice.

Edgar removed his suit jacket. "You make it by warming cream and then pouring it over chopped semi-sweet chocolate." As he spoke, Edgar hung the jacket over a nearby chair. Chunky gold cufflinks gleamed in the lamplight. "Then you mix the two together until smoothness is achieved. You can also add liqueurs if you have the inclination."

"I'll keep that in mind," Tree said.

"And the best news: I have found macarons here in Key West."

"That is good news," Tree agreed.

Edgar picked up the pink box and pulled at the ribbon until it came loose. He then raised the lid to reveal two neatly laid out rows of multi-colored macarons. "Let me see, which one will I try? What about you, Mr. Callister? What is your favorite?"

"I don't know."

"The salty caramel, lavender, or pistachio—what do you think?"

Tree didn't say anything.

Edgar plucked a purple macaron from the box. "I believe I will try the lavender."

He bit into the crunchy meringue shell, chewed reflectively for a moment and then with a sharp gasp of disgust, he spit out the macaron's masticated remains and simultaneously backhanded Tree across the face. "Where is it?" he demanded.

"Where is what?" said Tree, dazed, bending forward, holding his throbbing face.

"Where is my ten million dollars?"

"Ten million dollars?"

"Where is it?"

"I don't know what you're talking about. You're saying Elizabeth has stolen ten million dollars? Is that why you are looking for her?"

"The devil woman and the two idiots she works for."

"Miram Shah and Javor Zoran."

Edgar threw the rest of the macarons onto the floor. "This really is disappointing. If those are the best macarons Key West has to offer, I couldn't possibly spend more time here."

He pushed the lily away and picked up the machete.

The stinging sensation drifted off, but the side of Tree's face remained numb. He continued to hold it as he said, "I didn't know anything about the money. I thought Miram Shah and Javor Zoran were in love with Elizabeth. That's why they hired me to find her."

"Believe me this has nothing to do with love." Edgar stalked toward him, holding the machete. "Where is she? Where is the devil woman? Where is my money?"

When Tree didn't immediately answer, Edgar hit him again, much harder this time. The force of the blow rocked him back into the arms of the two henchmen who prevented him from falling to the floor.

"I am losing patience with you, Mr. Callister."

Unwanted tears sprang into Tree's eyes and rolled down his cheeks. "I don't know where she is."

Edgar slapped the flat edge of the machete blade against the tabletop. "Sometimes when I was a boy, we would go into a village, and we would do as many as one hundred short sleeves in an afternoon. Often we would become bored with the short sleeves and we would give out long sleeves. Funny, the things boredom makes you do, Mr. Callister. The ways you are willing to keep yourself entertained—do you cut off a man's arms or his hands? Which will it be? You would think these actions would deeply affect a person, but they don't. They become the things you do. So you see, it makes no difference to me whether you keep your hands. But it probably matters to you, so tell me where Elizabeth is, and I will let you keep at least one hand."

The two men shoved Tree hard against the table. Straw Hat grabbed his left hand. Tree tried to yank it away. Then the two simultaneously had a grip on him, pressing him forward, so that his elbow was on the table and they were forcing his arm out, palm up. His wrist, caught in the lamp-light, seemed thin and terribly vulnerable.

"Don't do this," Tree said. His voice sounded so high and hoarse, he feared Edgar might get the idea he was scared out of his wits.

"But this is what I do, you see." Edgar's voice, icily calm. "This is the weapon I employ to get what I want. What I want is that money and the devil woman herself, Elizabeth Traven. So I am going to give you one more chance to give me the answer I am looking for before I cut your hand off."

Amazing how little control he had over his body, Tree thought. As much as he fought against the pressure on his arm, he understood how totally powerless he was to do anything about it. "No," he shouted, as if that would do the least bit of good.

Edgar's arm rose, the machete in his fist, the blade gleaming in the light. Tree closed his eyes and gritted his teeth, trying to stifle the sobs bursting out of him, terrible sounds he could not control.

And then another voice said, "That's enough."

Tree blinked hard and squinted against the uncertain light. He couldn't see anything.

The voice reiterated, "Let him go, or I start shooting people."

Edgar very calmly said, "Who will you shoot first?"

"You, with the machete. The guy overdressed for the occasion. I'll shoot you first."

"It is called a cutlass," Edgar said.

"Who cares? Let him go."

The strong, binding hands slowly released him.

"Move into the light where I can see the three of you," the voice said. "Do it."

Edgar and his pals shuffled ahead so that the light struck them full on. Tree noticed that Pork Pie Hat had lost his hat. Edgar's face in the uncertain light was hard to read, and that made him even more dangerous in Tree's estimation.

"Tree," the voice said. "Come over here."

"Where are you?" Tree said.

"Just come toward me."

Tree wasn't quite sure his legs would support him. But as he wobbled forward, they held. He could see a shadow forming itself into a woman holding a gun with both hands. She moved as he came toward her and even in the hard light, Cailie Fisk's face held its angular beauty. Or was it Susan Troy's angular beauty? No matter. Whatever she called herself, she seemed to know how to handle a gun, and right now that's all that counted.

Edgar, still holding the machete, spoke calmly, as if to test the changed climate. "I think you won't shoot anyone."

"Is that what you think?" Cailie said. "That's fine. I'm a former St. Louis police officer. I've shot three people in the line of duty and to be frank, they deserved it a lot less than you morons. So do something stupid, and let's find out if I'm willing to pull the trigger."

No one moved except Tree who reached Cailie's side. Was that a Glock pistol she held so steadily?

"Tree," she said, "start moving toward the exit."

The order was promptly followed by a loud crash—the lamp hitting the floor.

The world plunged into darkness.

# 16

A hollow bang echoed through the darkness. It took Tree a moment to register that the sound came from a gun. A screamed curse was followed by the sound of scrambling feet. Coming toward him or running away? Tree could not tell which.

He called out Cailie's name. No reply. Maybe he got her name wrong. Maybe Susan no longer responded to Cailie.

Hands propelled him forward. He lunged through the black void he found himself in, feeling curiously claustrophobic, as though entombed in darkness.

Presently, a spot in the distance appeared, the blackness broken by a rectangle of gray. Tree plunged through it—diving into the rabbit hole. He found himself outside suddenly, the sketchy outlines of fishing trawlers, a tangle of masts draped in moonlight. Cailie was right behind him.

"Keep moving," she said in a breathless voice.

"Who did you shoot?"

"It was dark. I'm not sure I shot anyone. I've got a car over by the wharf."

The car was a gunmetal gray Yari hatchback. He squeezed into the passenger seat while she got behind the wheel. "Here," she said, handing him her gun. "Hold this."

He took the Glock while she started up the car. He worried that Edgar and his men would come charging and he would be forced to open fire. That's all he needed, dealing with the fallout from shooting someone in Key West.

But no one came after them as the Yari jumped forward, headlights capturing the hulls of dry-docked fishing boats, a section of chain link fence, and then open gates and a strip of roadway.

"How did you get here?" he demanded, cradling the Glock in his lap.

Cailie kept her eyes on the road. "Let's say I'm your guardian angel."

"Are you really a St. Louis cop?"

"If you don't mind my saying so, Tree, between throwing up on boats and getting kicked around by Key West thugs, I'd say you need help." She glanced at him and grinned. "You need another operative at the Sanibel Sunset Detective Agency.

"I wouldn't know what name to put on the employment form."

"We're both rather mysterious, I suppose. You don't know who I am. I don't know what you're up to in Key West that attracts the attention of gun-toting goons anxious to cut your hand off."

"Cailie or whatever you call yourself—"

"Call me Cailie. I don't want to make things too difficult for you."

"Look, I appreciate what you did for me back there. I'm not sure why, but you saved my hide. Now if you could just drop me off, I would appreciate that, too."

"Every time I think it might be possible that you're capable of dealing with the world you seem to involve yourself in, you reassure me you're not."

"Meaning what?"

"Meaning if I put you back on the street, what are you going to do? Chances are your pals back there are just going to find you again. And believe me, after what just went down, they will want to find you. This time they may do a lot worse than cut off your hand."

Tree had no choice but to see her logic. "What are you suggesting?"

"Go where they won't find you."

"Where is that?"

"With me."

"Not a snowball's chance in hell," Tree said.

"What choice do you have? Besides, we're the only two people in the world who are going to know anything about this."

"You're already making it sound as though we're up to no good."

She gave a snort of laughter. "You've just been kidnapped and beaten. I may have shot someone in a dark warehouse. And *now* we're up to no good? It's a little late to be worrying about that."

He heaved a sigh. "Where are you staying?"

"Not far away. The Casa Marina."

"What we will do," Tree said. "We'll go over there and see if I can get a room for the night."

"If that's the way you want it, Tree, fine."

———————

The hotel was full.

The desk clerk was so sorry, but everything was booked up. Tree was certain the clerk looked at him as if he was crazy not to stay with the lovely blonde beside him. Tree had to stop himself from blurting that he was a happily married man, and spending the night with this beautiful woman was the last thing in the world he wanted.

He had no choice but to follow Cailie through the long lobby, past the conventioneers crowding the bar area, everyone watching them, he was certain.

By the time they reached her room, he was dead tired. Kidnapping and threats tended to exhaust a detective—at least a detective of a certain age. The room, impersonal in shades of beige and ivory, was cast in a table lamp's burnished glow, illuminating the king-size bed turned down for the night.

"You said there were two beds," Tree said.

"I was mistaken," she said, tossing the key card onto the table and unslinging the large shoulder bag she had carried from the car, dropping it to the bed.

"I'll take the sofa," he said.

She laughed. "This is right out of a bad movie. Come on, Tree. You're bigger and older. You take the bed. I'll fit nicely onto the sofa. Are you hungry? Do you want anything to drink?"

"I'm fine," he said.

"Do you want to tell me why those characters were after you?"

"What difference does it make?"

She grinned and said, "Well, if I'm going to become another Sanibel Sunset detective in your organization, Tree, I should know what you're up to."

"I'm spending most of my time trying to figure you, Cailie."

Her smile widened. "I wouldn't waste my time if I were you. Trying to figure me out will only get you in more trouble than you're already in."

"You haven't told me if you're really a cop."

"It'll be on my resume when I apply for a job."

He was too tired to argue with her any more. He flopped onto the bed and was vaguely aware of her retrieving the shoulder bag and slipping into the bathroom. Exhaustion washed over him like a series of small blows. He propped his head against luxuriously soft pillows, and was sound asleep.

———————

Later—although how much later he could not say other than it was around the time he was being chased by the lion—he was shaken awake. Cailie Fisk's hair tumbled around her lovely, intense face. Was he dreaming? Hard to say.

"What is it?" he said.

Before he could stop her, she dropped her head to him, her lips finding his, savagely kissing him. He pushed her away. "I want you to know," she said.

"Stop this, Cailie."

"I'm going to destroy you and your wife—just like you destroyed me."

She kissed him again, and then she was gone. He tried to sit up and couldn't. It was a dream. Lions chasing him. Threatening women kissing him.

Bad dreams, that's all. If Freddie was here, that's what she would say.

He fell back to sleep.

# 17

When Tree awoke in the morning, he was alone in the room.

He had not heard a sound of Cailie leaving, and he still wasn't sure the kiss, and the threat that went with it, was anything more than a bad dream.

He got up from the bed, and padded into a tiled bathroom, so white its glare hurt his eyes. He stared at his bleary, unshaven face in the mirror. This morning he not only looked his age, he felt it, too. The muscles along his right arm and shoulder ached. He wanted to go back to bed and forget about everything.

Instead, he stripped off his clothes and ducked under the hot, reviving spray of the shower. That felt better.

He found a small bottle of mouthwash in the generous toiletries basket the hotel provided—just in case a guest arrived unexpectedly to spend the night with a mysterious woman who conveniently disappeared the next morning.

He tried on various scenarios that would explain to Freddie how he twice came to be in the same woman's hotel room. Even the truth came out like a lie. He inspected the one-day beard growth that on younger men made them look sexy; it made him look like Gabby Hayes—for those who remembered Gabby Hayes.

After he finished dressing, he decided to call Freddie and let her know he was all right. But not in the space recently shared with Cailie Fisk. He would wait until he was in the lobby. Somehow, anything he said would sound less duplicitous there.

Riding down in the elevator, Tree thought about how his mother and her sisters used to bring him and his cousins to Sanibel Island each winter. Occasionally, they would break up their stay with an overnight jaunt to Key West. He remembered visiting the Casa Marina, in awe of the grand old hotel built by Henry Flagler to house the very well-to-do arriving from Miami via his newly completed railroad. But Casa Marina had undergone renovation in recent years, and in the process its Old World charm had been lost. Now it was just another anonymously ultra-modern resort hotel.

In the nearly empty vastness of the lobby, Tree tried to use his phone, but could not get a signal.

He considered leaving Key West, taking a cab out to the airport and grabbing the first plane back to Miami. He would find a connecting flight to Fort Myers once he got there. But that would mean leaving empty-handed, and no closer to finding Elizabeth Traven than he was when he arrived. Had she really disappeared with ten million dollars? If she had, she wouldn't still be hanging around Key West.

Would she?

She might if Hank Dearlove was involved. Wherever Dearlove was this morning, maybe that's where Elizabeth could be found, too.

Outside, he found an available pedicab. The driver's name was Dominik. He was young and blonde and spoke with an American accent.

"I was born in Poland, though," Dominik explained as he started off. "But I've been here for a long time, so I guess that makes me pretty much American. You want to see where Hemingway lived?"

"You take a lot of people there?" Tree asked.

"It's unbelievable, man. Like what is it with the guy? He just wrote stuff, right?"

"You've never read Hemingway?"

"Reading, man. Get real. I play video games." Dominik laughed, like the whole idea of reading was beyond ridiculous.

Tree tried to imagine Hemingway playing a video game. He did not have that kind of imagination.

The day's first visitors were already streaming through the main entrance at 702 Whitehead as Tree's pedicab pulled up. Tree told Dominik to wait while he went to the ticket booth.

"Is Hank here?" Tree asked the young woman in the booth.

The woman checked a clipboard hanging from a hook on the wall beside her. She shook her head and said, "Hank's not scheduled today."

"He did such a great job yesterday I wanted to give him something. I'm leaving town today. Any chance I could get his address and drop it around to him?"

She shook her head. "I'm afraid we can't do that, sir. You can leave it with me in an envelope if you wish."

"I wanted to give it to him personally."

"I'm really sorry. We can't give out personal information."

Tree walked back to where Dominik waited at the curb. "Do you want to earn a quick twenty bucks?"

Dominik looked at him suspiciously. "Doing what?"

"Just go over there by the ticket booth and collapse."

"Collapse? You mean like fall down?"

"As though you passed out."

Dominik said, "Fifty bucks."

"What?"

"You want me to do something like that, it's fifty bucks."

"Done," Tree said. "Now get going."

Dominik eased off his bike. "What are you going to do?"

"I won't be far away," Tree said. "Just collapse. I'll take care of the rest."

Dominik held his hand out. "Not that I don't trust you."

"Twenty-five now," Tree said. "The other twenty-five when it's all over."

"Fair enough," Dominik said. Tree got his wallet out and put two tens and a five into the pedicab driver's outstretched hand.

Dominik stuffed the bills into his pocket and then walked briskly over to the entrance and stopped. He stood there and then his knees buckled, and he issued a loud gasp before dropping to the pavement.

Tree saw the woman in the ticket booth start and then call out, "Pete!" before she hurried out of the booth and rushed to where Dominik lay on the ground.

Tree crossed to the open ticket booth, and, as casually as he could, reached in the open window to lift the clipboard off its wall hook. Quickly, he scanned it. Dearlove, Hank. Thirteen William Street in Key West.

Tree returned the clipboard to its hook. He turned to see the young woman from the ticket booth and another attendant, presumably the guy named Pete, with Dominik who by now was sitting up. A small, concerned crowd had gathered around. Tree pushed through, announcing, "It's okay, I'll take care of him."

The young woman looked up at Tree. He could see the confusion on her face. With help from Pete, Tree got Dominik to his feet.

"Dehydrated," Dominik said.

"Still feel like driving me?" Tree said to him.

"No problem," Dominik said. "I'm okay now."

The young woman and Pete traded glances.

Back on the street, Dominik said, "How'd I do?"

"Award-winning," Tree said. "Billy Wilder said he could turn anyone into an actor. You're the proof of that."

Dominik said, "Who's Billy Wilder?"

"Can you take me over to William Street?"

"For another fifty bucks."

"Come on, Tree said. "Give me a break, will you?"

"It's the American way, man. Fifty bucks."

————————

Ten minutes later, Dominik swooped onto Fleming, crossing Duval before swinging left on William Street and arriving in front of number thirteen. Tree handed him the twenty-dollar bill they finally had negotiated. "Sure you don't want me to wait around?"

"I can't afford you," Tree said.

"I can make you a very attractive deal," Dominik said.

"I'm just a poor, starving tourist," Tree said.

"Sure you are, man. Getting guys to collapse onto the pavement for you? Come on. You're up to something that you shouldn't be, and when that happens, man the dollar signs start to fly."

"Is that the American way?" Tree said.

"What I came to this great country for."

"I'll be fine," Tree said.

Dominik looked disappointed, and Tree wondered how big a lie that statement would turn out to be.

The house, with its gleaming white verandas on the upper and lower levels, was set among lush palm trees behind a white picket fence, a fine example of the Queen Anne style that had arrived in Key West late in the nineteenth century.

Tree opened the gate and went up the walkway to the porch. He mounted the steps leading to the screen-door entrance. The inner door was open. From inside, Tree could hear the husky tenor voice of Tony Bennett.

Tree rapped on the screen door.

"Hello," Tree called. There was no answer.

Tree knocked again. Tony Bennett stopped singing. Silence, save for the insect sounds coming from the lush foliage crowding the house.

Tree opened the screen door and stepped inside, calling out again. His voice echoed through the interior. He stood in the entranceway, listening to the soft, motorized whir of an overhead ceiling fan. He called out a third and fourth time.

A ginger-colored cat padded along the main hallway running the length of the house. It was a Hemingway cat, Tree noticed, polydactyl, with six toes on each of its front paws. The cat spotted the intruder, and let out a loud meow, twitching its tail.

A tail brushed with crimson.

The cat twitched and turned back along the hall. Tree followed it into an octagonal-shaped, pine-paneled sitting room. Five shuttered windows filtered slivers of midday sunlight, outlining the overturned coffee table, the smashed lamps, torn-apart sofas and easy chairs, their stuffing scattered across the pine floor.

The same kind of damage had been done to a similarly paneled study with archways, featuring sunburst transoms, looking onto a pool area. A wood-carved desk had been up-ended. Various editions of Hemingway's novels had been yanked off the surrounding shelves and thrown haphazardly to the floor. Papers and files were strewn everywhere.

The cat stopped near a trail of red splotches leading onto the terrace. He let out another screech, his red tail twitching back and forth. Tree, now having trouble breathing, forced himself to follow the blood path onto a tiled pool deck surrounded by luxurious gardens.

Hank Dearlove's body lay at the bottom of the three steps leading down to the pool deck. Dearlove, in a flowered shirt similar to the one he had on the day before, lay on his back staring up at a cloudless sky he would never see again.

# 18

The ginger cat slithered against Dearlove's body, issuing another high-pitched shriek, its tail twitching, picking up more blood. Tree bent down beside Dearlove, pale and stiff on the terrace. Tree couldn't tell how long he had been dead or what killed him—but he was dead all right, no doubt of that.

Tree rose and went back inside the study to search for a telephone. The cat reappeared, calmer now, rubbing himself against Tree's thigh. Tree gently pushed him away, not wanting to be struck by that bloody tail. His gaze fell on the framed photographs adorning the walls: Hank Dearlove, crisp and pressed in a suit and tie, posed with a solemn-looking Vice President Dick Cheney. He shook hands with Defense Secretary Caspar Weinberger. He was part of a group of men posing at a cocktail party. Some of the men held up glasses and laughed into the camera. He recognized a younger, fitter Miram Shah and a burly Javor Zoran.

Tree looked around the room. Someone had yanked all the drawers out of the overturned desk, spilling its contents across the floor. Tree knelt to the mess of papers and books. Various letters and correspondence were addressed to HENRY DEARLOVE, ASSISTANT DIRECTOR, CENTRAL INTELLIGENCE AGENCY.

An antique telephone stood on a rosewood side table in the corner. Tree picked up the handset. As he did this, he spotted the brochure lying on the floor.

The Island Inn on Sanibel.

He called 911 and when the operator came on the line, he briefly told her what he had found at Thirteen William St. Then he hung up. By now he had some experience with these things. No use spending a lot of time on the line with 911 operators. The police would arrive soon enough.

Tree picked up the Island Inn brochure and went out onto the porch to gulp in a lungful of warm summer air. William Street for now was deserted. That was about to change. He leaned against the railing, staring at the bright, inviting photos contained in the Island Inn brochure: *A tradition since 1895.*

His phone began to vibrate in his pocket. He pulled it out. Now he had a signal. He looked at the readout on the screen: Freddie.

"Where are you?"

"I'm still in Key West," he said. "I called you earlier but couldn't get any service."

"So you're all right? I was worried."

He thought: I spent the night in another woman's hotel room, and I just discovered a corpse. Couldn't be better.

Aloud he said, "I'll call you later and fill you in."

"Okay, but are you still looking for Elizabeth Traven?"

"Yes."

"Well, she's not in Key West."

"How do you know?"

"Because I just drove past her on San-Cap Road."

As soon as the Criminal Investigations branch of the Key West police department identified the corpse in the house on William Street, the number of local police officers and Monroe County Sheriff's Department major crimes investigators increased exponentially.

Tree was interviewed by two detectives, Lieutenant Manny Valdez, who headed the department's major crimes unit, and Detective Nicholas Conde.

He gave the officers his narrow version of the truth: impressed with guide Hank Dearlove's insights during his visit to the Hemingway house, he decided to award Mr. Dearlove a bonus for his efforts.

When he arrived at the Hemingway house, he discovered Mr. Dearlove wasn't working. He happened to spot Dearlove's address on a clipboard, saw that it was nearby, and decided to go to his residence. When he arrived, the door was open and the bloody cat was wandering around. He went inside and found Dearlove's body out by the pool.

Simple, straightforward, and not too much of a lie. Neither Valdez nor Conde commented on his veracity, or his lack thereof. It was only when Conde asked him what he did for a living that the atmosphere changed.

"You're a private detective?" Lieutenant Valdez's voice contained a sharper edge. He was fortyish, heavyset, with black hair brushed away from a high forehead. He wore a sports jacket and a tie in a southernmost world where no one wore a jacket let alone a tie.

"That's correct," Tree said.

"Not around here."

"On Sanibel Island."

Lieutenant Valdez paused before he said, "I wouldn't have thought there is a lot of call for private detectives out there."

"There isn't," Tree said. "But once in a while, there is. That's where I come in."

"Are you here on a case?" Conde inquired. He was older than Valdez, slim, with a hard face that looked as though it had been cut out of stone by a high wind. He wore a short-sleeved, open-collar shirt, less formal than his boss without detracting from the impression he was the soul of rugged, military-type discipline.

"No," Tree said, trying not to take his eyes away from the two officers or do anything that would indicate he was lying through his teeth.

"You're not here on a case." Conde turned the question into a declarative sentence.

"No."

Conde again: "Then why are you in Key West?"

"A little sight-seeing overnight," Tree said reasonably. "I'm a bit of a Hemingway buff, but I'd never seen where he lived in Key West."

Conde sat back in his chair and said, "Hemingway," making it sound like a bad word. "I've never been able to get into Hemingway."

"No?" Tree tried to look interested.

"Everywhere you go in the Old Town, there are photos of the guy standing beside the biggest damned fish you ever saw. *The Old Man and the Sea?* I took that in high school. Old guy after a fish. I dunno. What's the big deal there?"

"Do you have any idea who this guy is?" An exasperated-sounding Lieutenant Valdez.

Tree said, "You mean Hemingway?"

Valdez jerked his thumb in the direction of the corpse by the pool, now covered by a sheet. "No, the guy out by the pool. Henry Dearlove."

"I thought he was a guide at the Hemingway house."

"Name doesn't ring a bell?"

"It didn't, no."

"You had no idea he was a former deputy director of the CIA."

"Is that what he is?"

"Yeah."

"How would I know that?"

Conde said, "Yeah, how would you?"

Valdez said, "Obviously, this is more than just some guy who leads tourists around by the nose over at the Hemingway place. There's going to be a lot of heat on me, on Nick here, on the whole department."

He leaned toward Tree, his face becoming tense. "That's why when some private detective from Sanibel tells us he just happened to be in Key West playing tourist, and he stumbles across the dead body of a big cheese at the CIA, naturally, Nick and I get a little suspicious."

"It might even cross our minds that you're not telling us the truth," Conde added.

"Why would I lie to you?"

"I don't know, Tree," Valdez said. "Why would you?"

"Listen, I had no idea who this guy was," Tree protested. True enough. "Like I keep telling you, I thought he was a tour guide. Does he still work for the CIA?"

"Apparently, he left five years ago," Valdez said. "Something about waterboarding Iraqi prisoners. I don't know why that would get you into trouble, but there you go."

The observation reduced the three of them to silence. Behind him, out by the pool, Tree could hear the murmur of voices: the crime scene investigative team at work.

"How did he die?" Tree asked.

"You're a private eye and you don't know how he died?" Conde sounded disgusted.

Tree delivered a blank look.

"Bang, bang," Valdez said.

"That means someone shot him," Conde said.

"I never get used to that police jargon," Tree said.

"Anything else you want to tell us?" Valdez asked.

"For what it's worth, I don't think you should waterboard people," Tree said.

Valdez studied him closely. "Maybe that's why you killed him. You don't like waterboarding CIA agents."

"He also thought *To Have and Have Not* was Hemingway's worst novel," Tree said.

"Yeah?"

"I would have said *Across the River and into the Trees*."

———

Tree could not face the Key West Express back to Fort Myers. Instead, he took a cab to the airport where he caught a 5:50 P.M. Capeair flight to Fort Myers.

During the flight, Tree tried to sleep but, in the cramped seat of the tiny Cessna, thoughts about why a former CIA deputy director who had been thrown out because he waterboarded people, was mixed up with Elizabeth Traven, not to mention Miram Shah and Javor Zoran, kept him awake. He refused to contemplate the consequences of withholding information about Dearlove's murder from the police.

His defense would be that he really knew nothing and therefore it was better not to say anything—not too far from the truth.

By the time he took a cab from the airport to the Key West Express, got the Beetle out of the parking lot, and drove to the island, it was after eight o'clock and nearly dark. As he came toward the house, the front door opened and Freddie stepped into view. She wore shorts and a T-shirt and looked wonderful. Tree was never so glad to see her. Then he saw the frown.

"Are you all right?" she asked.

"I got involved in something in Key West," Tree said.

"Yes," she said. "Some former CIA director or something. You found the body."

"How did you know?"

"The way I shouldn't know. I heard it on the news."

"I'm sorry," he said.

"Why didn't you tell me when I called?"

"I had just found the body. It didn't seem like the time, somehow. Let's go inside, and we can talk about it."

"There's something else."

"What is it?"

She held up a single sheet of paper. "This came today at work. It's from someone named Cailie Fisk."

His heart dropped into the pit of his stomach.

# 19

Dear Fredericka,

We have never met, but I feel I must write and tell you what has happened between Tree and me. While in Paris we ran into each other at La Closerie des Lilas. Tree and I ate dinner together that night, and, I am ashamed to say, we ended up back in my hotel room where he insisted on making love to me. I suppose it was mutual, I'm not sure.

Something powerful occurred that night. I'm not certain what— a combination of lust and guilt I suppose—but it was enough to draw me to Sanibel and back to your husband's side. He suggested we spend time together in Key West. He was going there on a case, anyway, and we would be alone and could get a better understanding of what was happening between us.

Again, I am not proud of this, but I accompanied him to Key West where we spent another night together. I'm not sure what I was thinking then, and I'm not sure what I'm thinking now. But you should be aware of what's going on.

I have urged him to think twice before giving up on a marriage and a life here on Sanibel. Maybe this letter will help clarify matters

*for all of us. But at this point, I must say, I find it hard to imagine
a life without Tree.*

*Sincerely,*

*Cailie Fisk*

Tree looked up from the letter, removing his reading
glasses. "She finds it hard to imagine a life without me?"

"Apparently," Freddie said.

"She's crazy," Tree said.

"Maybe you had better tell me who she is, Tree." Freddie sat with her legs crossed in a deck chair further away
from him than he would have liked. She tried to look relaxed but only succeeded in looking tenser.

"I wish I knew," Tree said. "She tells me her name is
Cailie Fisk. She told Chris that her name is Susan Troy."

"Chris? What's he got to do with this?"

"I think that's how she tracked me to Paris. She met
Chris about three months ago and got involved with him."

"Good grief." Freddie groaned.

"I did not sleep with her," Tree said. "Whatever her
name is, I didn't sleep with her."

"Then why does she say you did?"

"I don't know. I can't figure any of it."

"Why didn't you tell me what happened in Paris?"

"Because nothing happened in Paris."

"You didn't go back to this woman's hotel room?"

"Yes, I did."

She looked at him and he decided he had better tell her
everything. "She did come on to me, tried to kiss me. But I
stopped her and got out of there."

"Why didn't you say something?"

"Because I should not have been in her room in the
first place. I shouldn't have put myself in a spot where
whatever I said about it, it would sound suspicious. So I
decided the best thing to do was to keep quiet."

"Except here she is on Sanibel and here you are returning from Key West with her."

"I didn't go to Key West with her—or come back with her."

"But you spent the night with her."

He paused too long before he said, "Yes."

He saw the muscles in her throat tighten. "Did you sleep with her?"

"Did I have sex with her?" he said. "No. Nothing like that. But I had nowhere else to go."

Tree related how he found Hank Dearlove at the Hemingway home, his confrontation with him, his abduction later that night by Edgar Bunya and his thugs, Cailie's unexpected appearance, and how, fearing Bunya would be looking for him, he decided to stay with Cailie.

He then told her about going to Dearlove's house that morning and finding him dead from a gunshot wound. It was only then that he discovered Dearlove was a former CIA deputy director. A photo in the study showed Dearlove with Miram Shah and Javor Zoran, the two men who had hired him to find Elizabeth Traven. He now suspected the men were looking for Elizabeth because she had ten million dollars that belonged to them.

"Miram Shah held a high position in Pakistani intelligence," Tree said. "Javor Zoran ran security for Slobodan Milošević, and Dearlove was with the CIA. They all worked together. Then for various reasons, they found themselves out of a job, and somehow got together."

"To do what?" Freddie said.

"Whatever it is, it involves ten million dollars and Dr. Edgar Bunya and his cutlass."

"And now murder," Freddie said.

"Yes."

"Not to mention Elizabeth Traven."

"Who may be hiding out because she has ten million dollars that doesn't belong to her."

Freddie uncoiled her legs and leaned forward, those lovely green eyes unblinking, hard on Tree.

"You know what?" she said. "I don't believe you had sex with this woman. I really don't. There's too much between us for that; you're entirely too loyal. I may be crazy to believe, but I do. I believe it because I believe in you—in us."

She took a deep breath. "What I don't understand is why you wouldn't say anything, why you kept quiet about Paris. I know what you're saying, I hear the excuse, but it goes back to my continuing complaint about what you're doing. You're lying to me, withholding things, and I hate that more than anything."

"I know you do," Tree said.

"And yet you keep doing it."

Tree was silent.

Freddie rose to her feet. He got up, too, taking her in his arms, feeling her body stiffen against him. "You're still mad at me."

"I guess I'm not certain what I am. Disappointed is probably a better word."

And that cut him deeper than anything. He did not ever want to disappoint Freddie Stayner.

Yet that's exactly what he kept doing, he thought as he undressed. He looked over at the bed. Freddie was already asleep. He stood there listening to her soft breathing sounds before picking up his slacks off the floor. As he did this, something fell out of the back pocket. He stooped to pick it up.

It was the brochure from the Island Inn he had found at Hank Dearlove's place.

# 20

The next morning, Tree pulled up to the gates at Elizabeth Traven's home on Captiva Drive. If Freddie had spotted her, maybe she was back in residence.

But the house remained as silent and apparently deserted as ever behind its locked gates. This time when Tree called her cell phone number, an electronic voice told him the number had been disconnected.

As soon as Tree got into his office, he called Joseph Trembath. "Have you got news for me, Mr. Callister?"

"What do you know about a man named Hank Dearlove?" Tree said.

That prompted one of Trembath's silences.

"Mr. Trembath, are you still there?"

"Yes, yes of course I am. I'm just trying to understand what someone named Dearlove has to do with finding Elizabeth Traven."

"It may have something to do with the fact that I found Dearlove dead in his Key West home yesterday morning."

Instead of expressing surprise or shock, Trembath said, "Do you know where Mrs. Traven is now?"

"Are you listening to me? A man is dead. A man who appears to have been associated with Elizabeth Traven."

"I quite understand that," Trembath said in a neutral voice apparently unmoved by the news of murder—or by the fact that Elizabeth might be connected to it. "But that really doesn't change anything, other than to make it more imperative than ever that you find Mrs. Traven so that further complications can be avoided."

"What further complications are you talking about?"

Once again, Trembath chose to dodge the question. "Mr. Shah wants Elizabeth Traven found. That reality has not changed."

"Mr. Shah is a former director of the Pakistani Security Service is he not?"

Trembath said, "What has that got to do with anything?"

"Mr. Trembath, I know Hank Dearlove was with the CIA. I've seen a photo of him with Miram Shah and Javor Zoran. They are both looking for Elizabeth. The question is why?"

This time Trembath didn't even hesitate before he ignored the question. "Just find Mrs. Traven."

"You want me to find Elizabeth or do you want me to find the ten million dollars you think she stole?"

Yet again, Trembath betrayed no surprise when he said, "I'll call you at the end of the week. Do try to have some results. Time is growing short."

Trembath hung up. Tree replaced the receiver and sat back in his chair. He fished the Island Inn brochure out of his back pocket and laid it on the desk in front of him just as the office door burst open, and Chris Callister exploded in, flushed and out of breath.

"You bastard," he said, slamming the door.

He charged forward and for an instant Tree thought his son was going to punch him out. But Chris stopped just short of the desk, chest heaving, his pale face twisted into an expression of anguish.

"How could you?" he demanded. "How could you do it?"

"Do what?" Tree said, genuinely alarmed. "What did I do?"

"You slept with her, you slept with Susan."

"That's not true, Chris."

"I was with her last night. She was crying in my arms. Devastated by what you did in Key West."

"Nothing happened in Key West. No matter what she told you. Her name isn't Susan, incidentally. It's probably Cailie Fisk, although there is no guarantee that's true, either. Nothing about her is true. I don't know why she's saying the things she's saying, but I never touched her."

"You never spent the night in her room in Key West?"

"There's an explanation for that, if you sit down and listen to it."

"I don't want any more of your crap. That's all I've ever gotten from you. Either nothing—which is all mom ever got—or a lot of crap that turned out not to be true."

"Chris, think about this. Think about what you're saying. You know how much I love Freddie. You know I would never do anything to hurt her. You know that."

Chris stood there, his body trembling, Tree still uncertain if his son would hit him. Instead, he shook a finger at this father. "This is it with you. It's finished, I don't want to have anything more to do with you and your lies. Understand me? Nothing."

Chris retreated to the door. Tree jumped to his feet to block his exit. "Get out of my way," Chris said, curling a fist.

"Did you tell Cailie or Susan where we were staying in Paris?"

"I don't want to talk about this."

"Did you?"

Chris lowered his head, nodding. "We may have discussed it, I suppose."

"What about the kir royale and La Closerie des Lilas, did you talk about all that?"

"She wanted to know about you and Freddie."

"Look, there's something going on here. I'm not sure what it is, but this woman is not who she says she is, and for some reason she seems determined to destroy me, my relationship with you, and my marriage to Freddie."

"Any destroying that's going on, you're responsible for it."

"It's not just Key West. She followed us to Paris, too, and she was probably watching our apartment and tailed me the night I went to the Closerie. We had dinner and then I drove her back to her hotel. That's when she came on to me."

"You're lying!"

"Nothing happened. I left. The next thing, she's on Sanibel, and now she's even sent Freddie a letter claiming we are having an affair."

Chris's face had gone flat. "Susan wouldn't do that."

"Call Freddie, she'll confirm what I said."

"Lie for you, you mean."

"Yeah, right, nothing Freddie would like better than to protect me if she really thought I was having an affair. She's got the letter. She'll show it to you, if that's what you want."

Chris stood silently, not moving. Tree put his hand on his son's arm. He angrily shook it off. "Don't touch me!"

Stone-faced, Chris shouldered Tree out of the way and escaped out the door. Tree looked at his hand. It was shaking. Rex Baxter poked his head in. "Everything all right?"

Tree looked at him. "Why shouldn't it be?"

Rex shrugged. "It's just that there seems to have been a lot of yelling and screaming going on, tourists downstairs scattering for Naples."

"Sorry," Tree said.

"So everything's not all right," Rex said.

His son was sleeping with the woman who claimed to be having an affair with his father. Tree's wife was grappling with the notion that her husband was fooling around, determined to believe him but nagged by suspicions fueled by her husband's lack of communication skills.

What could possibly be wrong?

Aloud, Tree said, "Do me a favor will you? I need to find out if there is a woman named Susan Troy staying on the island. She may be using the name Cailie Fisk."

"This is the gal with Chris I met the other night at the Lighthouse."

"That's the one."

"Are you doing some sort of background check on her? Make sure she's suitable for your son?"

"Could you phone around for me?"

"Does this make me an official associate private detective?"

Tree smiled. "You're in charge of our fleet of boats."

# 21

Tree parked the Beetle in the Island Inn parking lot, and then went through the walkway onto a white sand beach where a series of white-painted clapboard cottages faced the gulf.

Just as he was deciding whether to check with reception before proceeding, Elizabeth Traven, wearing dark glasses and an electric blue one-piece bathing suit that made her shimmer in the sunlight, appeared in the open doorway of the nearest cottage—a goddess waiting on the doorstep.

She waved when she saw him and then stood waiting, one hand on her hip, until he came over. She did not seem all that surprised to see him.

"How did you find me?"

"Hank Dearlove left an Island Inn brochure lying around."

"Poor Hank," was all she said.

"So you know he's dead," Tree said.

"Why don't you come in out of the sun?"

Tree followed her into a sun-drenched sitting room. The white-painted furniture reminded him of the cottages his family occasionally rented on the island in the early 1960s. A flat screen television was the sole concession to the twenty-first century. Not exactly Elizabeth Traven's kind of place.

She swung around facing him, removing her sunglasses. The strains of disappearing had not disrupted her beauty. The incandescence of her swimsuit threw off unexpected heat. "I just came back from the beach," she said. "Can I get you anything?"

Tree shook his head.

"Well, now that I've been tracked down by that crack private eye, Tree Callister, I'm going to have a beer."

"Seems kind of down market for you, Mrs. Traven."

"I am a simple woman of the people, Mr. Callister," she said with a smile. "You should know that by now."

She swayed into the tiny kitchen to an old-fashioned refrigerator rattling away in a corner. She opened the door and bent to retrieve a can of Budweiser Lite. Faced with the view of her pear-shaped derriere, Tree was struck by the realization that once again he was alone with a woman without enough clothes on.

She straightened and snapped the cap on the beer, seeming to sense his unease. She smiled. "I'm making you nervous."

"You're making me wonder what's going on," Tree said.

"Are you sure you don't want anything?"

"Just some information."

Elizabeth perched on a sofa beneath windows that opened outward to allow a breeze from the ocean and the cries of children on the beach. He could hear himself a long time ago in those sounds.

He was distracted from his past by Elizabeth crossing the long legs that he used to spend far too much time trying not to look at.

"Why don't you sit down?" she said.

"Right now, I prefer to stand."

"In case you have to make a run for it?" Her smile brightened. "I'm not going to bite you."

"Every time I find a dead body, it seems you are not far away."

"You think I had something to do with Hank's murder?"

"Did you?"

She took a sip of her beer before she said, "I was a long way away when that happened."

"I'm guessing Dearlove realized a guy with a machete named Edgar Bunya was after you and decided he'd better get you out of Key West. Only you couldn't come back to your house, so Dearlove got you this place."

She drank some more of the beer.

"I take it from your silence you know who Edgar is," Tree said.

"We have met," Elizabeth acknowledged.

"Edgar jumped me last night and, when he realized I didn't know where you were, he went around to see Dearlove. When Dearlove wouldn't talk, Edgar killed him."

"How much of this have you told the police?"

Instead of answering, Tree said, "Miram Shah claims you're the love of his life. So does Javor Zoran."

That made her snort. "Miram is a fool."

"Funny, Hank Dearlove said the same thing before someone killed him."

"Well, it's true. He never should have hired you in the first place. He did hire you, didn't he?"

"So did Javor."

"Good grief." She rolled her eyes. "You've seen the two of them. What do you think?"

"Where you are concerned, Mrs. Traven, I'm never sure what to think."

"Well, I'm telling you they both have the wrong idea."

"Why do I suspect that if they do have the wrong idea, you gave it to them."

"That's not true."

"There is what you tell me, and then there is the truth."

"You were hired to find me. You've found me. Congratulations. Great detective work. Now you can report back. Mission accomplished, as they say."

"Except there is more to it," Tree said.

"Is there?"

"For instance, there's Edgar Bunya's money. What have you done with it?"

"I want another beer." But she didn't move.

"We don't have a lot of time for your games, Mrs. Traven. Edgar Bunya probably killed Hank Dearlove. I know he is looking for you. If I can find you, so can he. The police are going to be on me again today, and I don't feel much like lying to them again. So you'd better start telling me what you're up to."

"Oh, dear, Mr. Callister," she said with a mirthless smile, "I'm afraid you've learned something about the art of extortion since the last time we met."

"I've had a great teacher," Tree said.

"This started out purely as a business arrangement," Elizabeth said, and Tree believed for the first time that he had cornered her to the point where she had to talk. Whether or not there was any truth to what she was saying was something else entirely.

"I met Zoran at a party in Miami. He and Miram Shah along with Henry Dearlove had known each other over the years, from the time when Hank was with the Central Intelligence Agency."

"Zoran headed security for Slobodan Milošević. Shah was the deputy director of the Pakistani secret service. But by the time you met them, they must have been unemployed."

Elizabeth nodded. "Out-of-work spooks. What do they do with themselves?"

"What do they do?"

"They realize that in a world less and less friendly to despots, the kind of people they used to deal with regularly might be in need of the help that only they could provide."

"What kind of help?"

"Help getting into the United States. Hank came up with the idea that there might be a lucrative business in smoothing the way for various individuals with less than sterling credentials wanting to emigrate here."

"Legally?"

She waved a dismissive hand. "Strings are pulled. Money changes hands. But eventually, everything has to be done properly." She gave a wan smile. "Eventually."

"I don't understand where you came into all this," Tree said.

"They needed someone to liaise with their clients. It turned out that both Zoran and Shah were in this country under somewhat shaky circumstances themselves, meaning they were reluctant to leave. So they wanted an associate who had a clean record, internationally speaking, and who could speak to clients on their home ground."

"And collect the cash payments?"

"That was part of it, yes."

"Is that how you got your hands on the ten million dollars?"

"Ten million dollars? Where did you come up with that figure?"

"Edgar gave it to me."

"That's ridiculous," she said.

"Is it?"

She exhaled and uncrossed her long legs, a familiar maneuver that in the past had always worked to distract him. Not this time. "Mrs. Traven, I'm two seconds away from going to the police and telling them what I know."

She let out a groan, as though this was all too much for her. "All right. Do you know someone named Emomali Rahmon?"

"Should I?"

"He is the president of the Republic of Tajikistan, somewhat amusing since he isn't really a president and Tajikistan is not really a republic."

"What is Rahmon?"

"A ruthless dictator, but a *nervous* ruthless dictator, meaning he has seen the Arab Spring and a number of other events that don't bode well for the world's despots, and has decided the business of being a dictator is not what it used to be. He started looking for an exit strategy that would bring him to Florida where he has managed to bank much of his considerable fortune since coming to power in the early nineties. Hank Dearlove entered into negotiations. They sent me to Paris to pick up the down payment."

"Ten million dollars?"

"No," she said vehemently. "That was the eventual amount to be paid once Rahmon was successfully installed in a beachfront condo on Captiva Island. I never, ever, saw that kind of money."

"Why not simply wire-transfer the money into a friendly bank account?"

"Because these days there is no such thing as a friendly bank account. No, better for someone like myself, who doesn't create suspicion at borders, to collect the cash and bring it back."

"So then what happened?"

"I met Rahmon's man in Paris at the Georges V."

"I'm guessing Edgar Bunya."

She looked impressed. "Edgar is an international fixer, a man who gets the dirty things done for people like Rahmon."

"What rock did he crawl out from?" Tree said.

"A rock somewhere in Liberia. Edgar got his start as a child soldier for one of the warlords there. By the time he was a teenager, he had made enough of a reputation for himself that MI-6 decided they could put him to good use for some of the dirty work they needed done in that part of the world. They flew him to a special training center in South Africa, taught him how to speak English and how to torture people. When they didn't need him, they loaned him out to the CIA."

"Now he's graduated to the president of Tajikistan."

"He became too much for MI-6 and even the CIA. They cut him loose and he's been freelancing ever since." She gave another wan smile. "His specialty is not being nice. That's why people hire him."

"So you met Edgar in Paris. What happened?"

"He gave me the down payment—two hundred and fifty thousand dollars. Not ten million. Then I flew back to Key West and I gave Hank the money."

"So what makes Edgar think you stole ten million dollars?"

Her gaze was steady as it met his. "I have no idea," she said.

She's lying through her teeth, he thought.

"And why do you think Miram Shah hired me?"

"Didn't he tell you?"

"He didn't tell me the truth."

She shrugged. "I may have neglected to say I was flying to Paris."

"You mean Shah didn't know about the money Rahmon was supposed to pay you."

"That's a possibility."

"And neither did Zoran."

She looked at him.

"So unless I miss my guess, you and Dearlove hatched a scheme to keep the ten million dollars for yourselves. Only something has gone wrong."

"I keep repeating," she said patiently, "there is no ten million dollars."

"But something is wrong."

"Shah and Zoran turned out to be frauds—ruined men, desperate to keep themselves afloat. So they made promises they could not possibly keep. They could barely help themselves, let alone anyone else, and certainly not the president of Tajikistan. When he realized these guys couldn't do anything, he demanded his money back."

"But you and Dearlove decided to keep it for yourselves. And now Dearlove is dead and you're hiding out in case you're next."

"It's not true, but I understand that's what Shah and Zoran may be thinking."

"I'm going to the police," Tree said.

Elizabeth gave him a long, impatient look. "I don't think it's a good idea for you to get the police involved, Mr. Callister."

"Tough."

"Stay away from the police."

"Why should I do that?"

"Because if you do, I will tell you all about Cailie Fisk."

He looked sharply at her, trying to keep the surprise off his face.

Failing.

"What makes you think I want to know anything about her?"

"Come on, don't try to pretend she's not making your life hell."

"Don't tell me you're behind what she's doing."

Elizabeth shook her head. "And I'm not responsible for the Kennedy assassination, either."

"Only because you were too young."

"Do we have a deal or not?"

Tree glared at her. She beamed. Elizabeth—electric blue and triumphant.

As usual.

# 22

Tree phoned Rex as he walked toward his car. "What are you doing right now?"

"There are two naked women in my office," Rex said. "What are you doing?"

"Selling my soul to the devil," Tree said.

"That's how I ended up with my third wife," Rex said.

"How would you like to give me a ride in your new boat up to Useppa Island?"

"Given a choice between naked women and taking you up to Useppa Island, naturally, I would take you to Useppa Island."

"I'll meet you at the marina in an hour," Tree said. "Incidentally, I don't suppose you found where Cailie Fisk is staying."

"No one named Fisk or Susan Troy is registered at any of the resorts on the island," Rex said.

———

A gleaming white pleasure craft, sleek and shiny in the afternoon sun, roared past as *Former Actor* churned along Pine Island Sound.

Tree looked at Rex tensed at the wheel. He wore dark glasses and a lamp shade-shaped straw hat that made him look like a Mandarin peasant out for a cruise. He hunched forward to peer through the windshield, one eye constantly on the screen of the GPS unit he had installed after he ran aground the second—or was it the third?—time.

"We're going kind of slow," Tree said.

"I'm still getting my sea legs under me," Rex said in an edgy voice. "As long as we keep her between the buoys we should be just fine."

"And if we don't?"

"Then we do what I've already done a couple of times, we run aground. These waters are pretty shallow. Do you mind if I ask what we're doing out here?"

"We're two old friends out for an afternoon cruise together, off to talk to a Pakistani spy about his love life."

That made Rex take his eyes off the GPS screen for a couple of seconds. "I like the part about two old friends out for a cruise."

"What about the part where we talk to a Pakistani spy about his love life?"

"That part makes me wonder what the hell you're doing."

"You and Freddie," Tree said.

"Doesn't she know what you're doing?"

"More and more I think she embraces the idea of me not doing this."

"What? The new owner of Dayton's doesn't want you to get yourself killed?"

"How do you know about that?" Tree said, surprised.

"About getting yourself killed?"

"About Dayton's."

"I know everything," Rex said.

"Freddie wants me to run away from the lions."

"But you don't want to be Francis Macomber in that Hemingway story. You want to stand your ground and prove what a man you are."

"If I didn't know better, I would say you're siding with Freddie."

"Perish the thought," Rex said with a grin.

After an hour or so, the outline of Useppa Island appeared on the hazy horizon line. Closer, the gabled white rooftop of the Collier Inn came into focus. Tree directed Rex toward shore south of the inn, and Rex grew more nervous still, removing his sunglasses to more closely study the GPS screen.

"This is where it gets tricky," Rex announced.

"How does it get tricky?" Tree said. "You're headed for that long dock over there."

"It gets tricky if we run into a sandbar," Rex said.

Ahead, Tree could see movement on the dock where a low-slung powerboat was moored. As he watched, a couple of dark shapes pushed off the craft, its engines roaring to life. The bow rose high on the water before it came crashing down and the boat surged forward, coming directly for them at an alarming speed.

Rex swore and sounded a warning Claxton that howled across the bay but failed to deter the oncoming boat. Then, at the last possible moment, the boat veered left and came around the side of the *Former Actor*. Tree caught a glimpse of a muscular form in a white T-shirt aiming what looked to be a rifle.

"Get down!" Tree shouted.

Rex, at the wheel, looked at him blankly.

Something landed with a clatter on the *Former Actor's* rear deck, not far from where Tree and Rex stood. It bounced and rolled around before coming to rest against the stern.

"What the hell is that?" said Rex.

Tree yanked Rex off the captain's chair. Rex yelled, "What are you doing?"

"Get off the boat!" Tree said.

"What?" Rex said.

Tree wrestled him to the edge and pushed him over the side. He heard Rex holler something as he flopped into the water. Tree had a distinct memory of Rex bobbing in the boat's wake still wearing his Mandarin peasant's hat before putting his own foot onto the transom and launching himself forward an instant before the explosion erupted.

And the whole world turned red.

# 23

Tree under water, his mouth filling with the briny taste of salt water. His flailing feet struck sandy bottom—the bottom becoming a springboard he used to propel himself toward the surface.

When he broke above the waves, the view of the island and the hard blue sky was obscured by a black plume of smoke rising from the flames engulfing the *Former Actor*. Tree looked around, frantically calling Rex's name. A moment later, Rex's head broke the surface. Somewhere along the way, he had lost his mandarin's straw hat.

"My boat," he bellowed. "They blew up my boat!"

Already the *Former Actor* was settling into the water, stern down, emitting belching and gurgling sounds over the crackling of the devouring fire.

"Come on, Rex," Tree said. "Let's get to shore."

"They blew up the boat!" Rex kept yelling as if, otherwise, he would never believe it.

The swimming didn't last long. Their feet soon hit bottom and they were able to wade in the rest of the way. Shocked residents had gathered along the shoreline and huddled on the dock for a better view of the unfolding disaster. Helping hands pulled Tree and Rex onto the lawn fronting the houses. There was no sign of either Miram Shah or Joseph Trembath, the two people who should have been most interested in exploding boats.

Tree ignored everyone's worried demands to tell them what had happened. He heard Rex announce, "Somebody blew up my damned boat, that's what happened."

One of the onlookers became particularly excited. "Aren't you Rex Baxter? That guy who used to do the TV show in Chicago?"

Tree reached the steps leading to the porch of Miram Shah's house. He expected security guards to appear, demanding to pat him down, the same as the last time. This time, though, no one stopped him as he opened the screen door.

He called, "Mr. Shah? Are you here? It's Tree Callister."

There was no answer.

He stepped into the entry hall, closing the screen door behind him. He stood there, dripping wet, the silence of the house roaring back at him, much as it had at Hank Dearlove's place in Key West. Tree began to feel a similar sense of deep dread.

He forced himself along the passageway. Behind him, he could hear the screen door open and close. Rex said, "What's going on?"

Tree didn't answer. He reached a sitting room crisscrossed with impressive wood beams and big windows providing a panoramic water view.

Had he looked out one of those windows, Tree would have witnessed the final moments before the *Former Actor* disappeared beneath the waters of Pine Island Sound.

But Tree wasn't looking out the window.

His attention was focused instead on Miram Shah, naked, hanging from one of the beams. His head was at an odd angle, probably because of the piano wire tied around his neck. Rex stood beside Tree, looking up at the body. "Gawd almighty," he said in a low, wondering voice.

# 24

They blew up my boat!"
Rex kept reciting the same mantra to the detectives
from the criminal investigation unit of the Lee County
Sheriff's Department. It turned out they had jurisdiction
over boat explosions and murders.

*Why* exactly someone would blow up his boat was the
question Rex could not answer. He was not even certain,
he explained to investigators, what he was doing on Pine
Island Sound, other than the fact that his longtime friend
Tree Callister wanted a ride to Useppa Island, and he and
Tree had been friends for forty years, since way back in
Chicago when they were a whole lot younger, and they
didn't own boats that blew up.

It was left to Tree to explain what had happened. "A
grenade," he said.

The original detectives by now had been replaced by
the head of the criminal investigation unit, an intense,
iron-jawed recruiting poster for law enforcement named
Major Brent Lawson.

Major Lawson squinted at Tree and said, "Grenade?"

"At first I thought the guy in the other boat had a rifle he was pointing at us."

"A rifle."

"But then a grenade landed in the back of the boat. That's what exploded."

"Probably fired from a grenade launcher. Maybe an M32."

"You know about grenade launchers?"

"I'm ex-military," Lawson said. "M32 cartridge has a low-pressure chamber. Makes it almost silent. Forty millimeter grenade in all likelihood. High explosive fragmentation. Gets the job done. Why do you suppose anyone would launch a grenade at you?"

Tree thought of Edgar Bunya. The man in the white T-shirt on the other craft could have been Edgar or one of his men, and a fellow who would cut off your hand would certainly be capable of throwing a grenade at you.

Aloud, Tree said, "Maybe whoever it was had just killed Mr. Shah and thought we were attempting to stop him escaping."

"Were you?"

"Was I?"

"Attempting to stop him?"

Tree shook his head. "I was coming to see Mr. Shah."

"About what?"

"Like I told the other officers. I'm a private detective on Sanibel Island. Mr. Shah is—or was—a client."

Lawson said, "I didn't know there was such a thing as a private detective on Sanibel."

"There is. Me."

"So Mr. Shah had hired you." Lawson made it sound as though he had deduced this after clever questioning.

"Correct."

"To find this woman you told us about earlier?"

"Elizabeth Traven. He'd been involved in a relationship with her. He asked me to locate her."

"And did you?"

"Yes. She told me she wasn't interested in pursuing a relationship with Mr. Shah. I was coming out to the island to tell him that in person when this afternoon's events occurred."

"Do you know where Elizabeth Traven is now?"

"I don't," Tree lied.

"Any idea who would want to harm Mr. Shah?"

"Do you mean do I have any idea who would want to hang him by piano wire from the rafters in his own house? No. To me, he was an older man rather recklessly pursuing a younger woman who, it has become apparent, wants nothing to do with him."

It went on like that for another hour or so before everyone simply ran out of questions to ask—or maybe they got tired of hearing Rex going on about his lost boat. At dusk, a Sheriff's Department helicopter with Tree and Rex on board lifted off from the island. The crimson light of a failing sun illuminated the black oil patch marking the spot where the *Former Actor* went down.

As the green-painted chopper with "SHERIFF in big letters along its tail, swung south, Tree patted a forlorn Rex on the shoulder and tried to sound hopeful. "Maybe your insurance will cover it."

"Absolutely," he said. "There is a proviso in every boat insurance policy covering grenade attacks."

The chopper landed outside the Sheriff's Department headquarters at Six Mile Cypress Road. Freddie was waiting. "The two of you look as though you got blown out of a boat," she said.

"How did you guess?" Tree said.

She embraced him and said, "Are you all right?"

"I think so," Tree said.

"They blew up my boat," Rex said to her. Tree thought he might cry. Freddie embraced him too, and that seemed to make him feel better.

She invited him back to the house for dinner, but Rex declined. He just wanted to go home and get some rest.

They drove over the causeway onto Sanibel Island and dropped Rex off at his house. Tree walked him to the door while Freddie waited in the car.

"You sure you're going to be all right?" Tree asked.

"I'll be okay. I just need a little time, that's all. For you, this is business as usual, but for me, getting blown up and finding corpses hanging from the rafters, it's emotionally draining."

"I'm sorry," Tree said. "I shouldn't have gotten you involved in all this."

"I know this is a question Freddie has asked you before, but let me add my voice to the chorus wondering if you're sure you know what you're doing."

"The answer to that is no," Tree said.

Rex grinned and said, "Somehow I find that reassuring." Then, more seriously: "Watch yourself, okay? About the time the boat exploded, I began to get the distinct impression you are in over your head."

"Not me," Tree said. "You must be thinking of someone else."

"I don't think so," Rex said.

He gave Tree a look before going into his house and closing the door.

# 25

Tree stripped off his damp clothes and stepped into the shower. He stood under the hot spray for a long time, debating if he would ever leave. He couldn't get into trouble if he just stood here forever. Could he?

Don't be ridiculous, he concluded. Tree Callister could get himself into trouble anywhere.

Even in the shower.

By the time he changed into a short-sleeved shirt and a pair of shorts, Freddie had finished preparing her signature turkey burgers—filled with fresh, chopped basil, sun-dried tomatoes, crumbled goat cheese—accompanied by a spinach salad. They ate on the terrace, Freddie sipping a glass of wine. The familiar nighttime routine lulled Tree into believing everything was as it always had been, when in fact nothing was the same.

He told her about finding Elizabeth Traven at the Island Inn, the decision to go out to Useppa Island and confront Miram Shah. He told her about the powerboat, the grenade that blew up Rex's *Former Actor*, how they had swum to shore only to discover Shah's body hanging from a cross beam.

As he finished, the frown was back on Freddie's face— as it usually was when the twin subjects of Elizabeth Traven and dead bodies arose. Her burger was untouched. Only the wine received attention.

"How much of this did you tell the police?" she asked.

"I didn't tell them about Elizabeth Traven," Tree said.

"Why not?"

"Because she says she has information about Cailie Fisk and why she is harassing us."

That surprised Freddie enough to cause her to put the wine glass down. "You're kidding."

"I don't want to implicate her until I find out what she knows."

"She's blackmailing you—again."

From inside the house came the sound of someone pounding on the front door. "Who could that be at this time of night?"

"Elizabeth Traven?" Freddie said caustically.

Tree got out of his chair and went through the sliding glass doors into the kitchen. The pounding grew louder. He continued into the living room. "Who is it?" he called out.

"Police," a voice called out. "Open up!"

Tree unlocked the door. Sanibel Island Detectives Owen Markfield and Cee Jay Boone stood on the walkway. Behind them, Tree could make out half a dozen uniformed officers.

"Tree Callister," Markfield said in a brittle, formal voice, "I'm looking for your son, Chris."

Tree looked past Markfield to Cee Jay. She averted her gaze. Cee Jay had put on quite a bit of weight since the last time he saw her. Everything strained against the dark blue pantsuit she wore.

"He's not here." He could sense Freddie behind him.

"We want to come in and look around," Markfield said in the official voice of authority young police officers tended to use to make themselves feel more important. Markfield was blond and good-looking and, in Tree's estimation, an officious jerk. The grave authoritarian tone fit him perfectly.

"Do you have a warrant?" Tree demanded. Topping the list of questions he never thought he would ask.

"Do we need one?" Markfield said.

Tree traded glances with Freddie. She moved her head slightly. Tree turned to the detectives. "Come in. Take a look around."

He stepped back to allow the blue herd inside. Tree confronted Cee Jay with yet another question he never thought he would ask: "Is Chris under arrest?"

"We just want to talk to Chris," Cee Jay said.

"Call him on the phone. You don't need to send a platoon of cops after him at this time of night."

"Come on, we're wasting time," Markfield growled.

Cee Jay nodded to the men and they immediately spread out through the house.

"We'll be out by the pool when you're finished," Tree said.

Fifteen minutes later, Cee Jay came out without Markfield to where Freddie and Tree waited. "Do you have any idea where your son is?" she asked.

"I thought he was at his apartment or working," Tree said.

"He's not at the Holiday Inn and he's not at his apartment. When was the last time you saw him?"

"I spoke to him this morning at my office."

"If you're talking to your son again," Cee Jay said, "it's important that he contacts us as soon as possible."

"He didn't kill his wife, Cee Jay. The case was closed. What's happened to change that?"

"Just make sure he calls or comes in to police head-quarters."

Cee Jay turned and left.

"Were we ever in Paris?" Freddie asked wistfully.

They were, Tree thought. But that was trouble, too.

# 26

Freddie, as usual, was awake at six the next morning. Tree, as usual, stumbled out of bed, found the worn cargo shorts he liked to wear, and lurched into the kitchen to make coffee for Freddie. He no longer drank coffee. It didn't agree with him. Nothing did these days, not coffee, not booze, not rich food or meat. He ate minimally, drank nothing, but still he felt crummy.

He fought off the feelings of anxiety and depression that arrived with increasing regularity. What was wrong with him? The dead bodies he kept finding, the son accused of murder, the thugs trying to cut off his hands, people who launched grenades at him, the lies women told him, the lies he told the woman he loved. Maybe all those things had something to do with this morning's misery.

By the time the coffee was ready, he was feeling pretty sorry for himself.

Freddie entered, setting the kitchen aglow in something cool and light by Eileen Fisher. Freddie most definitely was not feeling sorry for herself today. Or any day, for that matter. She wouldn't allow that. You got on with things.

You did not sit around brooding. Tree swore he would take a page from her playbook.

Soon.

"How are you doing Tree?"

"Actually, I was thinking about you. In the midst of all this, I never asked where you and your investors are with Vera and the Dayton stores."

"Well, I wouldn't say we're exactly moving forward."

"No?"

"Mrs. Ray is having second thoughts. At least that's what she's telling us."

"You think it's something else?"

"I don't know what to think. I suspect it's real. That she is hesitating to give up the connection to Ray's memory. But I'm not sure. She's hard to read."

Freddie put the untouched coffee on the counter and glanced at the wall clock. "I'd better get out of here. I've got an early meeting with my people."

"With your people?"

She grinned. "The people with whom I am associated in this potential acquisition. We have to go over strategy and decide on next steps."

"I'm sorry, my love, I haven't been much help to you lately."

"As long as you're okay."

"I'm fine. As soon as I get into the office, I'm calling Edith Goldman, alert her to what's happening to Chris."

"Are you worried the police are looking for him and he has run away?"

"I'm afraid he's not thinking straight, about me or anything else right now."

She came and wrapped her arms around him, and then held his face between her hands. "Promise me you're going to be careful, darling. There are a lot of dangerous things going on here. Promise you will think before you act and not do anything rash."

"I'm calling Edith Goldman. How rash is that?"

She kissed his mouth. "I'll see you tonight?" With a hopeful question mark attached.

"Of course." He held her tight against him. "I love you," he said.

"I know you do, Tree. I know you do."

He noticed she didn't say "I love you" back.

———

Tree stopped at the Island Inn on his way to the office. He walked around to the cottage where Elizabeth had been staying. The place was locked. When he checked at reception, he found that she had left the evening before. When he tried her cell phone, the electronic voice reminded him that the number he was calling had been disconnected.

The parking lot at the Chamber of Commerce Visitors Center was full when Tree got there. The tourist season was in full swing. He finally found a space at the rear and entered the building. Rex wasn't in his office. One of the volunteers said he was downstairs in the main reception area talking to tourists—Rex's favorite pastime. Probably regaling them with stories about being blown out of his boat, Tree thought.

The reception area was jammed with tourists, talking to volunteers, poring over maps, lining up for the rest rooms that were the most popular stop when arriving on Sanibel Island. One of the volunteers finished providing directions to the Mucky Duck, the landmark bar and restaurant on Captiva Island. "Have you seen Rex?" Tree asked.

The volunteer said, "He was here a couple of moments ago."

Then someone gasped.

And someone else screamed.

Tree turned to see a man lurch through the shifting, panicking crowd. He was unshaven, in a rumpled linen shirt and baggy gray pants. Tree pushed through the crowd and broke into an open space created by onlookers jerking reflexively away as the man collapsed to his knees, hands pressed against his stomach, the linen shirt turning red.

The man fell face forward. Tree, dropping to his knees, managed to catch him before his head smashed into the floor.

The man looked up at Tree, and Tree looked down into the pale, anguished face of Javor Zoran. His lips opened. He was trying to say something, but no words came out.

Then the light went out of Javor Zoran's eyes, and he died in Tree's arms.

# 27

Javor Zoran had driven his 1983 Jaguar XJS as far as the parking lot at the Visitors Center before he stumbled out, leaving the motor running, and staggered inside where Tree had cradled him while he died from a gunshot wound to the stomach.

Self-inflicted? It was hard to say, according to Detective Owen Markfield and his partner, Cee Jay Boone. No gun had been found in the car. It was also hard to say where Zoran had driven from. He may even have crossed the causeway in that condition. They would be checking the video cameras at the toll booths.

Tree was not much help, but then he never was, Markfield observed caustically. Markfield's dislike was plain as he consulted a thick notebook.

"You have been busy since I last saw you, Callister, finding bodies all over the west coast. We've got a report from the Key West sheriff's office. Another from the Lee County sheriff on Useppa Island. And now here we are today. The bodies keep piling up. You're our local Dead Body Guy aren't you?"

If Tree had been a really good private detective, he would have cracked wise, as in the hard-boiled detective novels he read as a kid. But he couldn't think of a line wise enough to crack. He never could at times like this. Some detective.

Even Markfield appeared to expect Tree to say something and looked uncomfortable when he didn't. He covered up with another glance at his notebook.

Cee Jay chimed in: "You knew the victim?"

"Yes, Zoran was a client."

"So he was coming to see you with a bullet in him."

"He could have been, I don't know," Tree said. "I happened to be in the reception area when he stumbled in. One of the volunteers or a tourist was just as likely to catch him as me."

"But if he didn't want to see you, why would Zoran come here?" This from Cee Jay.

"Maybe he wanted a map of the island, I don't know."

Tree's cell phone trembled in his pocket. He fished it out. He did not recognize the number on the digital readout. "Excuse me," Tree said to the detectives. "I have to take this."

Elizabeth Traven said, "Are you alone?"

"No."

"Police?"

"Yes."

"You haven't told them about me, have you?"

"Not yet, no."

"Do you know Pete's Time Out in Times Square over at Fort Myers Beach?"

"Yes."

"I'll be waiting there in one hour."

Tree looked at Markfield and Cee Jay. "If there's nothing else, I have an appointment with a client."

"There's plenty more," Markfield snarled.

"Then it will have to wait," Tree said, standing.

Markfield stood facing him. Cee Jay said in a warning voice, "Take it easy, Owen."

Markfield plastered on a tight smile. "I don't know what you're up to, Callister. But I'm going to find out, and if you're lying to us, I'm gonna make sure you go to jail for a long, long time."

Tree swallowed and said, "Excuse me, Detective, but you're blocking my way."

Markfield slowly moved aside to allow Tree out the door.

———————

Tree managed to get Edith Goldman on his cell phone as the Beetle crawled over the San Carlos Bridge, caught in vacation traffic choking the roadway onto Fort Myers Beach.

"What kind of trouble are you in now?"

"And good afternoon to you, too, Edith," Tree said. "What makes you so certain I'm in trouble?"

"What? You're leaving your wife and phoning me for a date?"

"If that ever happened, Edith, you would be first on my list."

"Now I know you're in trouble. What's up?"

"For the time being, anyway, it's not me, it's my son, Chris. The police were at my house last night looking for him in connection with the murder of his wife."

Edith took this in for a moment before she said, "I thought that matter was resolved."

"Apparently not."

"Have they arrested him?"

"They're looking for him. They say they only want to talk to him, but judging by the heavy artillery they brought around, I suspect they're going to make an arrest."

"Where is Chris now?"

"I don't know."

"You don't know? Or you don't want to say?"

"I don't know where he is, Edith."

"You think he's on the run?"

"I hope not."

"All right," Edith said. "As soon as he turns up, have him call me. I'll take him over to police headquarters. But don't let him go over there alone."

"Okay. Thanks, Edith."

"I keep hearing about you and dead bodies."

"The police call me the Dead Body Guy."

"Well, be careful," Edith said. "We don't need the father and the son in jail. It gets very expensive for Freddie."

Tree finally got across the bridge and found a space in a parking lot off Fifth Avenue. He walked over to Times Square where kids on spring break and middle-aged midwesterners seeking relief from the cold, cold north jammed the pedestrian walk. Self-conscious fourteen-year-old girls wore patches of cloth they must have had to smuggle past their parents. The guys ambled along in basketball jerseys and flat-peaked caps, fake gangstas stalking budding supermodels.

Melon, owner of Pete's Time Out, held court at one of the tables outside his cottage-like restaurant. Melon originally was from Chicago and knew both Tree and Rex back there. Melon had a real name but no one could ever remember it. He was simply, Melon. His face under his ubiquitous baseball cap, framed by a neatly trimmed beard, lit up as he embraced Tree.

"Good to see you, partner," Melon said.

"It's been a while, Melon," Tree said. "I'm meeting a friend."

"Sit down, man, make yourself at home. You still on that Diet Coke shit?"

"You got it, Melon."

"You need a beer, man. You're not Florida and sunshine unless you got a beer in your hand."

"Even with a beer, I'd doubt I'd be Florida and sunshine."

"I know, man. You're Chicago, through and through. Can't change that, no matter how long you bake under the sun."

Melon grinned and went off to find Tree his Diet Coke. Across the street, a trio of teenage girls tried on sunglasses. Next door at a jewelry stand, a couple of women inspected earrings. The women stopped looking at the earrings to gaze admiringly at Elizabeth Traven as she swept out of the crowd toward Tree.

If she was hiding out, she was doing a lousy job of it. She moved with liquid grace in a pair of white shorts that, combined with the high-heeled Manolo Blahniks, reminded the passing parade that mature beauty always trumped youth.

Elizabeth presented Tree with a distracted smile before plunking herself down next to him, pushing her sunglasses up into a soft nest of hair. Unblinking opaque eyes studied him.

"How are you, Mr. Callister?"

"Not particularly good," Tree said. "Every time I turn around, I find another dead man associated with you."

As if objecting to talk of dead men, she shifted her face away and lifted it to the sun. "You keep saying that. I wish you wouldn't."

"This morning, Javor Zoran came into the Chamber of Commerce with a bullet in his stomach. He died in my arms."

Melon returned with Tree's Diet Coke, eyes riveted to Elizabeth. Tree introduced them. Elizabeth ordered a gin and tonic.

Melon asked, "You folks want to see menus?"

Elizabeth shook her head distractedly.

"Just the drinks for now, Melon," Tree said.

Melon went away. Elizabeth focused on Tree. "Before he died, did he say anything?"

"What if he did?"

"I would like to know."

"He didn't mention his great, lost love Elizabeth Traven, if that's what you mean—or ten million dollars for that matter."

She made a face. "You're being nasty."

Melon was back with her gin and tonic and a couple of menus, "just in case you folks get hungry."

He cast a final appreciative glance at Elizabeth before making his departure.

She looked at the gin and tonic in its frosted, perspiring glass. Tree said, "You don't seem too upset that he's dead."

"Maybe I'm very good at hiding my emotions."

"I'm thinking whoever killed Zoran, also killed Hank Dearlove and Miram Shah."

"Is that what you think?"

"Looking for that missing ten million dollars."

She lifted up the gin and tonic. "How many times do I have to tell you? There is no ten million dollars."

"Then Dearlove, Shah, and now Javor Zoran, died for considerably less. But nonetheless, they are all dead, and maybe you're running scared, thinking you could be next, and that's why you called me."

"No offence Mr. Callister, but if I was looking for protection you would not be the first person I would call."

"Except maybe you're running out of people. Everyone you know seems to be dead."

"I'm telling you, that's not why I called."

"Then why did you?"

"We had an agreement, remember?"

"You were going to tell me about Cailie Fisk."

"In return for not saying anything about me to the police."

"What is it you know, Mrs. Traven?"

"What about the police?"

"Your name hasn't come up."

She took a strengthening sip of her drink before she said, "Cailie is Kendra Dean's sister."

Tree looked at her in astonishment. "She's the sister of my son's murdered wife?"

"Cailie Dean is her real name. She is a detective with the St. Louis Police Department, although she's taken a leave of absence."

Tree's throat felt constricted. He could barely bring himself to spit out the words that formed his next question: "How do you know this?"

"Some time back, Cailie came to see me."

"How long ago?"

"About three months."

The same time Cailie became involved with Chris, Tree thought. Before he and Freddie left for Paris.

"She had questions about the affair Ray Dayton had with Kendra," Elizabeth continued. "The affair that led to her sister's murder. She wanted to know about Ray's suicide. She found it too convenient that the police had hung her sister's murder on a dead man. She had questions about

Chris. She demanded to know what I knew about all this, about Ray, and about Kendra and Chris."

"What did you tell her?"

Elizabeth shrugged. "I said I found it hard to believe Chris would kill his wife. He had already made his deal with the devil as far as Kendra was concerned. I'm not even certain how much he knew about Kendra and Ray."

"Obviously, she didn't believe you."

"Obviously not."

"Did she know Freddie and I were going to Paris?"

Elizabeth thought about this before she said, "She may have. She gave me the impression she'd done a fair amount of poking around—that she knew a lot more than she was letting on."

"Did she say anything about what she planned to do?"

"No, but she made it clear that if I said anything to you, she would come after me, and that would be, to quote her, 'a world of trouble you don't want right now.'"

"So why are you telling me, Mrs. Traven?"

As I told you, we had an agreement. That agreement has now been fulfilled, don't you agree?"

"Which means?"

"You don't have to follow me around." She looked at her watch. "I've got to go. Can you afford to buy me a drink?"

Elizabeth didn't wait for his answer as she stood. Tree said, "What about you? What are you going to do?"

"Don't worry about me. I'll be fine."

"Will you?"

"Let's face it. Just about everyone who might have wanted to harm me is dead."

"Edgar Bunya isn't. In fact, just the other day I think he fired a grenade at me."

"But he missed."

"Barely."

"Stay away from me, Mr. Callister. It will make life much easier for both of us."

She gave him a vague smile and walked away. Tree watched her retreat until the gleam of those long legs was lost in the crowd.

"Now that's a woman."

Tree turned to find Melon with a silly grin on his face. He might have argued the point, but what was the use? That perception had served Elizabeth well all her life and perhaps even allowed her to get away with murder.

# 28

Edith Goldman got hold of Tree a couple of minutes after he crossed the bridge onto San Carlos Boulevard.

"The police have arrested Chris," she said.

"Where did they find him?"

"Apparently he was coming to work at the Holiday Inn. I happened to phone Cee Jay Boone to check out the lay of the land. They were just bringing him in. Cee Jay says they've got new evidence supplied by a St. Louis police detective."

"That's Chris's sister-in-law—Kendra's sister," Tree said.

"You're kidding," Edith said. "How long have you known this?"

"I just found out myself. Where are you now?"

"I'm over here at police headquarters."

"Have they charged him?"

"Not yet."

"Okay," he said. "I'm just coming out of Fort Myers Beach on San Carlos Boulevard. Depending on the traffic, I should be there in twenty minutes."

It took him over half an hour with the traffic coming onto Sanibel and then more traffic backed up along Periwinkle. He finally got off onto Dunlop Road and into the city hall complex that housed police headquarters. Edith Goldman waited in the main reception area. In the sort of dark business suit seldom seen on the island, gripping a Blackberry as though it were a life raft, Edith looked sleek and professional, the sort of person you want at the jail when they are holding your son. "I was just about to call you," she said.

"What's happening?" Tree demanded.

"They've just charged Chris with the first degree murder of his wife."

"Oh, God," Tree said.

Edith said, "It's all right. We're going to take care of this."

Cee Jay Boone, looking rumpled and tired, chose that moment to appear, a tote bag slung over her shoulder, car keys in hand. Tree intercepted her. "I want to see my son," he said.

Cee Jay gave him a dead-eyed look. "I can't let you do that, Tree."

"Yes, you can," Tree said. He saw Edith out of the corner of his eye. She did not look happy. "You can do this for me, Cee Jay."

"I don't have to do anything for you," she said.

"Do this," he said. "Please."

She looked at him angrily. "Careful, Tree. There are a lot of people here who would love to see you in a cell right next to Chris."

He met her gaze. The anger did not go out of her face. "Five minutes," she said. "That's it."

Without another word Cee Jay led him down a short hallway and opened a door into the same interrogation room Tree previously had occupied—the father and son suite at police headquarters. Chris, haggard and hollow-eyed, sat with his hands handcuffed together, head lowered, as if in prayer. His son in handcuffs, Tree thought. The end game for the number of ways he had screwed up with him over the years.

When Chris raised his head, Tree saw the tears in his son's eyes. "They're saying I murdered Kendra, Dad. They're saying I killed her."

"I know," Tree said. "I got here as soon as I could."

"I didn't kill her. Tell them that. Tell them I didn't kill her."

"We're going to get you out of this, Chris. I promise you. Whatever it takes, we'll do it. We'll get you out of this."

"You know I didn't do it, don't you, Dad? You know I couldn't hurt her, no matter what happened. You know that."

Momentarily, Tree wondered if Chris wasn't melodramatically playing to the video camera that almost certainly was recording the scene. He dismissed the thought and said, "Yes." But did he? Of course he did. His son was innocent. Concentrate on that. His son was innocent.

"We don't have a lot of time," Tree continued. "Have you had a chance to talk to Edith?"

The question made Chris pull himself together. He sat up straighter, taking a deep breath. "Briefly," he said. "I'm going to be arraigned tomorrow."

"I'll be there," Tree said. "As long as this takes, no matter what, I'll be there for you."

Chris looked suddenly anxious. "Have you heard from Cailie?"

"Cailie?" Tree said in a tone that suggested she was the last person he expected to hear from. "You know about her? You know who she is."

"I know what they're telling me." Chris sounded more weary than surprised.

"You had no idea she was Kendra's sister?"

"They didn't get along. Cailie was critical of what Kendra was doing—or wasn't doing. The two of them had stopped talking. You know we got married in Las Vegas, just the two of us. No families. I don't think I ever saw a photo of Cailie. They say I confessed everything—whatever everything is—to Cailie. That's so crazy."

"Do you need anything?" Tree asked. "Is there anything I can do for you?"

Chris leaned forward, his face taking on an intensity Tree had not seen before. "Please, Dad, contact Cailie. Tell her I understand what's going on, I do. It makes no difference. We can get past this. Tell her that, please. I don't hold any of this against her."

Tree stopped himself from blurting, "You've got to be kidding"—perhaps because he had enough self-awareness to recognize that his son was not the only male in the family who fell victim to beautiful, lying, coldly manipulative women.

Instead, he said, "Do you know where she's staying?"

"She's rented a condo over at Sea Bell Road by Blind Pass. Talk to her, Dad. Make her understand that I still love her."

"Do you think that's the best thing right now?" Tree said, choosing his words carefully. He felt as though he was crossing a minefield every time he opened his mouth in front of Chris.

"It's the only thing," Chris said vehemently. "It's all that counts."

# 29

It was dark by the time Tree turned into the condominium complex where Chris said Cailie was staying on Sea Bell Road. He parked the Beetle feeling tired and depressed, wondering what he was going to say to her. "My son still loves you even though you've just had him arrested for murdering your sister?"

That didn't sound quite right.

A black Ford Fusion shot into view and slammed to a stop. Sanibel Island Detective Owen Markfield opened the driver's side door and jumped out.

"What do you think you're doing, Callister," he said. Markfield looked smart in a navy blue Polo shirt that hugged his slim torso.

Caught by surprise, all Tree could say was, "Detective Markfield."

"Answer me," Markfield ordered. "What are you doing here?"

The muscles rippled beneath his Polo shirt. He looked ready for a fight.

"I don't think that's any of your business," Tree said.

"If you're here to harass Ms. Dean then it is my business—it's police business. Now tell me what you're doing here, otherwise I'd be happy to talk about this at police headquarters."

"I want a word with Cailie."

"She's under police protection," Markfield said. "You're not going anywhere near her."

"It's all right, Owen," Cailie said. She had come out of the passenger side of the Ford, dressed head to foot in black, her hair pulled into a bun, accentuating the lines of her clear, lovely face.

"You don't have to deal with this jerk," Markfield said.

Cailie did not take her eyes off Tree when she said, "Owen, why don't you wait for me at the apartment?"

Markfield appeared to have difficulty getting his head around the idea. He nodded slowly. "Any trouble Cailie, you just call out. Hear?"

"Park in front," Cailie said. "I'll be along shortly."

Markfield gave Tree a dark look before swaggering back to the Ford Fusion. He climbed inside and drove away.

Tree stared at Cailie. "Don't tell me, you and Markfield—"

"Just two police officers bonding together over a particularly difficult case." She smiled. "Are you jealous, Tree?"

"I think the word is amazed," he said.

"Owen believes I need protection."

"But we know better, don't we, Cailie?"

"In Owen's immortal words, what are you doing here?"

"I know who you are," Tree said.

"Good. That makes things easier. What amazes me is why it took you so long to figure it out."

"Well, it's as you said, maybe I need another Sanibel Sunset detective to help me with these things."

"I'm afraid I'm no longer available," Cailie said.

"No, I guess not."

"Despite myself, I kind of like you, Tree. I started out hating you because as far as I could see, you had protected Chris, helped him lie to the police about my sister. Kendra and I never got along. All our lives we were very different people. I despised what she became, but she didn't deserve to die. She was my sister, and she was dead and I was sitting there in St. Louis not doing a thing about it."

"So you decided to do something," Tree said.

"I was angry. I wanted to destroy you, and your wife, too."

"So you arrived on Sanibel, found out where Chris was working, checked into the hotel and arranged to meet him."

"That part was easy enough," Cailie said. "Chris was very anxious to forget about his poor dead wife, and tell me all about his father, and the trip to Paris he was going to take with his wife Freddie, how much he liked the Closerie des Lilas and kir royale."

"Chris loved Kendra, he wouldn't hurt her," Tree said.

"I might even have believed you. As difficult as I made things for you, I might have believed you in the end—until Chris started talking too much."

"He convinced you that he killed his wife?"

"Something like that, yes."

"I don't believe it," Tree said.

"That's understandable. The point is, the police and the district attorney, do."

Tree gritted his teeth. "I came over here because Chris wanted me to talk to you."

She said nothing, and in the darkness it was hard to see if there was any reaction.

"He believes the two of you can get past this."

He expected a derisive laugh, but all she said was, "We probably can—as soon as he spends the rest of his life in prison."

"That's not going to happen," Tree said.

"There is a confession—recorded."

"A confession from Chris?"

"I've already said too much."

Tree said. "As long as there is breath in me, I'm going to fight to make sure he doesn't go to prison."

She shook her head. "Then I don't have anything to worry about, do I? At the rate you're going, there's not going to be any breath in you for much longer."

# 30

When Tree finished telling Freddie about Cailie Dean, she said, "I suppose that explains why she was in Paris and then in Key West coming on to you."

"It doesn't really explain much of anything," Tree said. "She does things to destroy our marriage and then she saves my life. Right now, none of it makes any difference. What matters is that she could put Chris in jail for life."

Freddie put her hand gently on Tree's knee. "You are not going to want to hear this. But you may have to deal with the fact that Chris did say something incriminating to her—and she did record it."

"I was there, and I know he didn't kill his wife," Tree said.

"You were there, and you covered up for your son and arranged things so that it looked as though you might be the killer. I wonder if that's blinded you to what may have actually happened."

"No," he said angrily.

She leaned back, removing her hand from his knee. "I hope for Chris's sake you're right."

They stood at the same time, and he wrapped his arms around her. She nestled against him. "Oh, Tree," she said. "Oh, Tree."

"I know," he said. "I know."

She pulled away from him. "It's probably a lousy time to bring this up."

"What is it?"

"They want me to fly to New York in a week or so and meet with some investment bankers and some of their SMEs."

"Their what?"

"Subject matter experts."

"What are they?"

"In this case, specialists in putting a deal like this together and stick-handling it through the banks.

"I thought your investors had the money."

"No one *has* anything, as such. What they have is the ability to raise money. At some point everyone has to go to the bank. We are at that point."

"Of course," Tree said. "Do what you have to do."

"I don't like the idea of leaving you right now," Freddie said.

"I'll be all right," Tree said.

Lying through his teeth.

———

Tree's eyes shot open.

He found himself staring at the ceiling, wide awake. He could hear Freddie's gentle breathing beside him in the darkness.

He got out of bed, feeling more anxious and uneasy than ever. He went out of the bedroom and found himself on a wrought iron walkway over a sun-dappled courtyard.

Tree crossed the walkway to an open door that led into an office with an antelope head mounted on the wall. A big man wearing shorts and a loose-fitting shirt stood writing at a lectern. He had dark hair and a mustache.

The man looked up from what he was writing and said, "Have you figured it out yet?"

The question surprised Tree. "Figured out what?"

"Why you've spent so many years following me around?"

"You know about that?"

"You've been at the house where I was born in Oak Park. The finca outside Havana. I'll bet you even ordered one of those Papa Doubles at La Floridita."

Tree looked embarrassed.

"I can't even remember inventing the damned thing," the man said. "Either I was too drunk or it didn't happen. Personally, I favor the not happening."

"I'm in an awful mess," Tree said.

"I know," said the big man. "When you're anxious and worried, you start looking for the heroes from your youth in hopes they can help. Well, Tree, old pal, I wish I could help, but I can't. At the end of the day, I'm just a writer. I stand here in the mornings with a stubby pencil and I cover pieces of paper with words. That's all I do. In the afternoon I drink and get mixed up with the wrong women. I've got no particular insight into anything."

"But you represent a certain demanding masculinity where things such as bravery and drinking and being able to use your hands when it comes to a fishing rod or a gun, matter," Tree said.

"Are you trying to suggest they don't?"

Tree shook his head "That's the problem, I secret-ly believe they do, but I'm no good at any of that stuff. When Francis Macomber showed cowardice in the face of the charging lion, his wife despised him and went off and slept with the white hunter—the guy who stood his ground. That story has stuck with me all my life. I don't care what women say. They are drawn to the white hunter who doesn't run from the lion."

"So you think your wife is going to go off and sleep with a white hunter, is that it?"

"I see the look in her eyes lately. She's after bigger things—a chain of supermarkets. She could end up very rich. She looks at me and what does she see? A failed news-paperman playing at being a detective—and not a very good detective at that. Not a good father, either. He can't even help his own son. Who could blame her for sleeping with a white hunter? Although, I've got to confess, I'm not sure there are a lot of white hunters around the Sanibel-Fort Myers area."

"Well, I've buggered things up with women by and large, so I'm probably not the right fellow to be talking to, but maybe you've got to have more confidence in her," the man said. "My biggest mistake, I believe, was that I did not trust the women in my life. I thought that if I didn't shoot the lion, they would think I was a coward. What I didn't understand is that they weren't interested in me shooting a lion. They could care less."

"What did they want?"

"The one thing I didn't give them enough of," he said.

"What was that?"

"Love, old pal. You can gamble for money and you can gamble for gold. But if you haven't gambled for love and lost, then you haven't gambled at all."

"You've got to be kidding," Tree said. "That's from an old Frankie Laine song."

"Never heard of him," the man said. "What I say to you is true at first light. After that, though, who knows?"

"I come to you looking for help and you quote Frankie Laine?"

"Who's Frankie Laine?" a voice said.

Tree opened his eyes and said, "You don't know Frankie Laine?"

"The singer? You're dreaming about Frankie Laine, the singer?" Freddie's confused, lovely face loomed over him. "It's time to get up. You're going to miss Chris's arraignment."

# 31

At 10:30 A.M. Chris, in shackles, and outfitted with a prison-issue orange jump suit, was arraigned at the Criminal Division of the Lee County Courthouse in downtown Fort Myers, charged with murder under section 782.035 of the Florida Criminal Code. Chris, without his glasses, looked pale and unshaven, like someone, Tree couldn't help thinking, who might have killed his wife.

In a badly fitting blue blazer he hadn't worn since his *Tribune* days, and a tie Freddie thought she had thrown away, Tree sat in the spectators' gallery with Freddie holding his hand. Cee Jay Boone passed, jerking her head up and down, her idea, Tree supposed, of a morning greeting. There was no sign of Cailie Fisk.

Edith Goldman asked for a bond hearing to set bail. The judge, a veteran of the local bench named Floyd Lallo, set a date for the following week.

The whole procedure lasted only minutes, everyone going through the motions without emotion, as though it could matter less, when in fact a young man had been accused of the worst crime of all, and his life hung in the balance.

Tree tried to catch his son's eye as sheriff's deputies escorted him out, but Chris stared straight ahead. Maybe Chris blamed him for all this; maybe Chris was counting on his dad to do a better job of protecting him, and he had failed.

In the corridor outside the courtroom, Tree asked Edith about the possibility of bail. "We'll have to see. The prosecution will argue they had to go looking for him so he's a flight risk. On the other hand, Chris has stuck around for months and didn't try to run away. So we'll see."

"We'll get the money," Freddie interjected decisively.

"Have you heard anything about the evidence they have against him?" Tree asked.

Edith shook her head. "We don't have the discovery yet. They'll put that off as long as possible."

"Supposedly Chris confessed to the murder," Tree said.

"To this Cailie Dean. Apparently she's a detective with the St. Louis police."

"And Kendra's sister," Freddie added. "Isn't there an argument to be made that whatever she got from Chris was coerced or there was entrapment—something?"

"Let's see what they've got first, and then we can make some decisions." Edith spoke in her irritatingly non-committal, professional lawyer's voice.

Tree walked Freddie back to the lot across the street from the courthouse. When they got to her car, she hugged against him. "It's all so cold and impersonal, isn't it?"

"Surreal," Tree agreed. "As though you're watching a bad movie full of actors who aren't very convincing."

"Listen, they want me in New York tomorrow."

"Okay."

"I'm going to have to fly out this afternoon. Are you all right with that?"

"Of course. There's nothing much you can do here for the moment. How long will you be gone?"

"Three or four days. Depending on how the meetings go."

"Good luck," Tree said.

"Thanks," she said. "I'm probably going to need it."

They kissed. A perfunctory kiss? Distracted? Hard to tell. Tree didn't want to read too much into it. But as Freddie got into her car he feared there was a distance between them that had nothing to do with the miles between Sanibel and New York City.

———

At the office, Rex entered bearing lattes.

"You're a lifesaver," Tree said, accepting the cup.

Rex plopped himself down in the chair across from Tree's desk. "How did it go?"

"As well as you might expect when you're sitting in a courtroom watching your son in shackles being arraigned for the murder of his wife."

Rex sipped at his coffee. "You think you've got trouble. I just got off the phone with my insurance company. Guess what? My policy doesn't cover grenades blowing up a boat."

"I feel terrible about what happened, Rex," Tree said. "Really, I do. I'm going to make this up to you, I promise."

"You've got enough to deal with right now," Rex said. "Let me worry about the boat. You take care of Chris."

"I haven't done a very good job of that, either. What do you do when you're son is charged with murder?"

"You believe," Rex said. "You believe he didn't do it. You hang onto that."

"That's what I'm trying to do," Tree said.

"I'm here if you need me. Anything, anything at all, Tree. You know that." Rex stood up, looking unexpectedly embarrassed. "And that's the last time in this friendship I'm going to be serious."

"I appreciate that," Tree said, grinning.

"We get too serious and we might be overtaken by real life, and we wouldn't want that."

"No way," Tree said.

"That real life is a killer," Rex said.

Vera Dayton appeared in the doorway. Hiding his surprise as best he could, Tree said, "Vera."

"Hey, there, Vera," Rex said.

"I was just passing by," she said.

"Yes."

"Have you got a moment?"

Rex disappeared. Tree rose awkwardly. "Come in and sit down."

She was done in island chic this morning: white slacks with matching white jacket over a scoop-necked blouse in silky blue; no sign of the drunk from their previous encounter in the well-to-do woman who gazed uncertainly at Tree as she seated herself.

"I heard about Chris—his arrest."

Tree felt his stomach drop. "Yes," he repeated.

"I thought you should know, I've just come from the police. I told them I don't think your son killed his wife. I believe, as I have always believed, that it was Ray."

"What did the police say?"

Her eyes darted around the office, as if the answer might be somewhere in the picture of the marlin on the wall. Finally deciding it wasn't, she said, "They asked if there was anything I wanted to add to what I had already told them. I said, no. But I asked them to keep in mind that Ray committed suicide, that if he had not murdered Kendra, there was no reason for him to take his own life."

"Look, I appreciate this, Vera," Tree said. "I know it's very awkward for you to talk about this."

"I don't know why they had to reopen it," Vera said, sounding abruptly agitated. "It had been settled. We're all trying to get on with our lives. Now the nightmare starts up again."

"I'm afraid it does," Tree said.

"Do you have any idea what evidence they have?"

"Not really," he said, not wanting to tell Vera any more than he had to. Not that he knew much, anyway.

The telephone rang. Tree looked at it.

Vera got to her feet. "I should be going."

"No, it's all right, Vera. They'll leave a message."

It rang again.

"There's something else I wanted you to know."

Tree looked at her. Again, her eyes nervously swept the room. Tree said, "What is it, Vera?"

"I'm not going to sell my stores to Freddie and her group."

"You know I'm not involved in this," Tree said.

The telephone kept ringing. Vera's voice rose over the sound. "Of course I know you're not involved. How could you be? What would you know about it? What does anyone know about it?" She sounded angry. "I've thought about it long and hard. I'm not selling. I'm not going to do it."

"Please," Tree said, "You should talk to Freddie. She's on her way to New York, but you should talk to her."

Vera said, "I shouldn't be here. I've got to go."

And she left the office.

The phone rang again. Tree grabbed the receiver.

"Hey, man, it's Melon."

Tree silently groaned. Melon was the last person he wanted to talk to today. No, he was the second last. Vera was the last, but it was too late for her.

"Melon."

"Wow, I just heard about your son on the car radio. That's pretty heavy, man. I just wanted to call to say how sorry I am."

"Thanks, Melon, I appreciate that."

"If there's anything I can do, you let me know, okay?"

"Right now, there's not much. We're just hoping we can get him bail next week."

"I was talking to Liz about you last night," Melon said. "She was saying how much your son means, and that you'd been through a lot together."

Tree gripped the receiver tighter. "Liz?"

"Sure, man. Liz"

"You mean Elizabeth Traven?"

"Yeah, Liz. She dropped in for a drink."

"I'm trying to get a line on where she's staying."

"I think Captain Rick has a bit of a crush on her."

"Captain Rick?"

"He owns half the properties around Times Square. He let Liz use the apartment. Gave her a terrific deal on the place."

---

The apartment was located above a T-shirt shop fronting Times Square, the entrance reached via a flight of stairs at the rear of the building. Tree stood on the beach facing a sand-colored façade edged in turquoise. A big towel adorned with skull and crossbones hung from a balcony railing. Blinds covered the second floor windows, so it was hard to tell if anyone was home.

Elizabeth Traven didn't want him following her. The agreement between them had been fulfilled, she said. What was that supposed to mean? Any time Elizabeth declared herself in that way, Tree could be sure there was something behind it. Was the ten million dollars inside that apartment? Is that why she didn't want him hanging around? Tree resisted the urge to go up there and find out. Instead, he occupied one of the picnic tables at a nearby beachside café. He ordered a Diet Coke from the waiter, keeping an eye on the apartment.

The Spring Break crowd streamed between the beach and Times Square as the afternoon wore on, and the sun gradually lost its battle with gathering clouds. The wind grew in intensity causing the multi-colored flags dotting the sand to flap violently. Attendants began taking down blue beach umbrellas. The rising wind drove all but the most dedicated bathers off the beach so that as dusk fell, the wide stretch of sand running past the pier was deserted.

Tree was standing, trying to get the kinks out of his tired body, when the door at the top of the stairs opened, and Elizabeth Traven stepped onto the balcony. For one stomach-dropping moment, Tree was certain she had spotted him. But then he saw that she was on a cell phone, looking into the distance.

Presently, a blue Mazda came into view and parked on a strip of roadway adjacent to the beach. A woman got out of the car and waved up to Elizabeth who immediately put her cell phone away and waved back.

Tree watched as Cailie Dean started up the stairs.

# 32

As soon as Cailie reached the landing, Elizabeth turned inside. Cailie followed her.

Ten minutes later the door opened, and Cailie re-emerged lugging a green L.L. Bean duffle bag. Elizabeth was right behind her, carrying a similar bag. Elizabeth paused to lock the door while Cailie continued down to the car.

Tree watched as Cailie opened the trunk of the Mazda and threw the duffle bag inside. A moment later, Elizabeth added the second bag and Cailie closed the trunk.

Cailie squeezed behind the wheel while Elizabeth joined her in the passenger seat. The engine started up and the Mazda drove off. Tree hurried around to where the Beetle was parked, hoping the women were headed across the San Carlos Bridge and he could pick them up there. Sure enough, as he swung onto Fifth Avenue, he spotted the Mazda on the bridge.

Tree topped the bridge as the Mazda turned into the marina just beyond Doc Ford's Restaurant. What were they doing there? Tree wondered. But then what were they doing together in the first place? He couldn't begin to imagine.

By the time he turned into the marina, the Mazda was already parked. In the gathering gloom and the rising wind, he watched Elizabeth and Cailie lug their duffle bags along the dock to a cabin cruiser. They stowed their gear below decks before returning to the car and driving away.

Tree waited until the car reached San Carlos Boulevard and disappeared before going along the dock to the cruiser. The boat was a thirty-eight-foot Sea Ray Sundancer. Tree climbed onto the rear deck, and went through the cockpit and stepped down into the cabin area, luxuriously appointed in ivory and brown with a stateroom off the main salon. The identical green L.L. Bean duffle bags lay on one of the leather sofas. He wondered if they contained ten million dollars.

The twin bed in the forward stateroom was occupied by a long white vinyl bag, containing what? A sleeping beauty? Not quite. When Tree undid the side zipper, the flap peeled away to reveal the serene face of Edgar Bunya, his eyes open and staring in blank wonder at Tree. One hand was positioned on his chest, clutching a Calla lily, the sign of Edgar's friendship. Edgar, however, would make no more friends, and he would never threaten anyone with a machete again.

Tree quickly re-zipped the bag.

Then he returned to the salon where the duffle bags lay. He opened one of them. Instead of ten million dollars, he found a Glock entrenching tool made of black polymer with a spade-like pointed blade, a thick coil of rope, and two Pelican flashlights with rubberized handles. The other bag was empty.

Tree closed up the duffle bags and then heard a noise above. He ducked into the stateroom. Presently, footsteps thumped against the deck.

"All right, let's get going," he heard Elizabeth Traven say.

"You sure you know how to handle this?" Cailie's voice.

"I grew up on boats," Elizabeth said. "I've handled bigger than this."

"It's starting to get rough out there," Cailie said.

"We'll be fine."

"You need anything below?" Cailie's voice.

Tree tensed.

"No, help me cast off, and let's get going."

He heard the satisfying growl of twin engines starting up. The craft shuddered and then began moving, backing out of its dock space. The roar of the engines increased as the throttle was thrown forward. Tree heard one of the women say something, but couldn't make out what it was.

As the boat picked up speed, the ride abruptly became rougher. Tree braced himself.

The motion of the boat as it entered the roiling waters of the gulf caused Edgar's body to shift around on the bed. The wind rose into a high-pitched shriek. The craft rode onto the crest of a wave and then plummeted into the trough.

Tree's stomach did a somersault. He tried not to think about sea-sickness.

Wind and waves shook the boat. This time Tree's stomach executed a cartwheel. He broke into a sweat. Edgar's body slammed against the bulkhead.

His stomach dropped again. Tree staggered from his hiding place and got to the sink in the galley kitchen in time to throw up. He tried to retch quietly, but it didn't work.

Cailie's frowning face soon appeared in the hatchway. She scrambled down the steps.

"That's a relief," she said. "For a moment there, I thought Edgar had returned from the dead."

She raised her hand so that Tree could see the Glock. "Is that the same gun you used to shoot Edgar?" Tree said.

"It's indiscriminate. That's what I love about the Glock. It will shoot anyone. So don't do anything stupid."

"I'm too sick for stupid."

"My experience with you, Tree, is that nothing keeps you from stupid. Otherwise, you wouldn't be here. Do me a favor. Raise your hands."

Tree thought of any number of smart replies to that cliché but decided against all of them. He raised his hands. She moved forward, gun at the ready, to pat him down. Rather professional, he thought, as she plucked his cell phone from his pocket.

"I'll hold onto this," she said.

From above Elizabeth's voice called out, "What's going on?"

Keeping her eyes fixed on Tree, Cailie yelled back, "We have a stowaway."

"What?"

"Tree Callister's come for dinner."

Elizabeth's disbelieving face, streaked with rain, popped into view. "Tree, good grief, what the hell are you doing here?"

Another wave smashed the boat causing Edgar to hit the bulkhead with renewed force. Elizabeth's head disappeared. Tree groaned and slumped forward.

"Stay put," Cailie yelled.

"Shoot me," Tree said. "Anything's better than this."

"I'll shoot you later," Cailie said. "Right now, I need you to pull Edgar up onto the deck."

"Why do you want me to do that?"

"He needs air. What do you care? Just do it."

"What happens if I don't?" Tree said.

"We'll find room for you in that body bag," she said.

"I'm interested in how long you've been involved in this."

"I'll bet you are."

"I'm thinking it's from the time you first went to Elizabeth asking about your sister."

"Tree quit talking and lift up the body."

"Elizabeth probably saw the same things I saw: someone with a gun in a world of people with guns who could take care of the things she couldn't take care of." He nodded at the body bag. "Like Edgar here."

"Pick him up, Tree," she said.

"There aren't a lot of people I would have put up against Edgar, but you would certainly be one of them, Cailie."

"I'm not going to tell you again." This time there was a nasty edge to her voice.

Tree couldn't think of anything but to go along and perhaps delay the moment when Cailie would decide to put a bullet in him. If Edgar Bunya, with his machete couldn't beat her, how could he?

For now, he wouldn't think about that.

His stomach twisted again and he dashed to the sink, expunging green bile—all that was left in his system.

"What's the matter with you? You're always seasick," Cailie said disgustedly. "How do you live in South Florida?"

"Uneasily," Tree said.

Feeling even weaker and more nauseous, he turned back to the body and, with some effort, pulled if off the bed. Edgar, Tree decided, was not going to go easily into a bad night.

"I'll need help," Tree said.

Cailie looked even more exasperated. "God, you can't even move a body by yourself. What good are you?"

"After I'm on the deck, you prop up Edgar so I can pull him up."

"All right, but hurry."

Tree managed to clamber up the steps, despite being thrown around by the rocking boat. When he poked his head out the hatchway, he was hit by a blast of wind and rain. He took deep gulps of refreshing, salt water-saturated air as he lurched onto the deck.

Despite its size, the Sea Ray was a cork being tossed around in hell's washing machine. Tree caught a glimpse of wind-flattened wave-tops in a storm-filled darkness before turning his gaze to Elizabeth. She was a sight, soaked to the bone, seated in the cockpit chair huddled over the wheel, fighting to keep the wildly yawing boat on course, eyes fixed on the glow of the GPS screen in front of her. Outside that tiny glow, the world was pitch black. How could you have any idea where you were headed on a night such as this? "You're crazy," Tree called to Elizabeth. But either his words were lost in the wind, or she chose not to hear him.

The boat shook from the force of another wave, knocking Tree hard against the hatchway. He looked down to see that Cailie had managed to get Edgar upright against the stairs. Tree grabbed the body bag with both hands.

"Can you lift him up a bit?" Tree called.

"Hold on," she said. "Let me get myself properly positioned."

Cailie had no compunction about wrapping her arms around Edgar's corpse and lifting it up, while at the same time Tree got a better grip on the vinyl material and pulled hard. Edgar reluctantly rose upward. A lot more pushing and pulling was required on both their parts to get Edgar out the hatchway onto the rolling deck. The rain against the vinyl bag made a sound like exploding firecrackers.

Cailie came up through the hatchway, unperturbed by a dead body or the howling fury of the storm.

"Get him over the side." Her voice was strong and clear above the wind.

"I don't want to do that," Tree said.

"Yes, you do, Tree." The raised gun was a kind of punctuation.

Tree bent down to once again take the edges of the body bag and pull it to the stern of the boat. In order to get Edgar over the side, he had no choice but to hook his hands under Edgar's arms inside the bag and hoist him up. Edgar through the vinyl felt loose and malleable. Rigor mortis had come and gone. Edgar had been dead for a while.

Tree got him up onto the stern and then did more pushing and pulling until the body finally dropped to the swim deck. It rolled back and forth a couple of times but didn't go into the sea. Tree was sure he would have to somehow get down to the lower deck and push it off. Then a big wave slapped against the boat, rocking it violently, and the glistening white body bag was gone.

He heard Cailie say something. Tree twisted around in time to see her lunging at him. For an instant, he was certain she was going to shoot him. Instead, she made a sudden flicking motion with her Glock hand. The barrel clipped his head and, amid starbursts, he leapt into the black, rainy void of the night.

# 33

Tree regained something like consciousness, soaking wet, his head hurting, his stomach aching. When he tried to sit up, he discovered his hands had been handcuffed behind him. He lay on his side on the cabin floor, steady beneath him, the pounding seas finally at rest. He silently promised whatever gods controlled these things that if he ever got off this boat in one piece, he would dedicate his life to being the good boy his mother always said he could be if only he would just do as he was told.

"Take it easy, Tree." Cailie's voice came from somewhere behind him. "We'll be docking in a few minutes."

Tree tried without much success to twist around to her. "What are you doing?"

"Be quiet Tree or I will shoot you."

"You're always so calm when you threaten me," Tree said.

"I'm calm because I know what I will do," she said. "You should know, too."

"Come on, you wouldn't shoot me, would you?"

She smiled. "You'd better shut up."

The boat's engines gurgled into neutral. Tree felt the boat nudge against what he assumed was a dock. They had landed. But where?

He heard the shuffle of feet going up the ladder. He strained around and saw that Cailie had left the cabin, and he was momentarily alone. The air filled with the sweet, sickly smell of his vomit. He struggled around and managed to get himself upright.

He was sitting like that when Cailie reappeared. "I thought I told you not to move."

"You told me to take it easy."

She stepped past him and grabbed one of the duffle bags and heaved it up through the hatchway. She did the same thing with the other bag.

Then she turned to Tree, leveling the gun at him. "Stand up."

Tree pushed himself against the bulkhead and used it as leverage to propel himself into a standing position. The effort sent stars spinning and dancing before his eyes. Dimly, he heard Cailie tell him to go up the stairs. He wasn't sure he could do it since his legs felt rubbery. He stumbled up the steps, fell forward and then crawled onto the deck.

The night was calmer, the wind having died down, but the sky remained dark and full of threatening clouds. The boat swayed gently, secure in its slip. Elizabeth Traven, framed by shore lights flaring out of the darkness, said, "I don't believe this."

"What don't you believe, Mrs. Traven?" Tree said.

"I don't believe how stupid you are. I tried to warn you to stay away. Why couldn't you just leave well enough alone?"

"Maybe I just had to see you drive a boat through a storm at night."

"Impressive, don't you think?" Elizabeth said.

"I wouldn't have thought you could do it, but I should know by now that when you are desperate, there is nothing you won't do."

Cailie came up on deck. She said to Elizabeth, "Why don't you put the bags in the car while I keep an eye on our friend here."

Elizabeth didn't argue. She picked up the bags and carried them off the boat. Cailie, meanwhile, knelt to Tree. "Okay, Tree, there's a car not far from the dock. We're going to walk to it, and you are not going to give me any trouble, do you understand?"

"Where are we?"

She stood, shaking her head. "Anything you need to know, I'm going to tell you. Right now all you have to do is keep your mouth shut and get to the car. Okay?"

He struggled to his knees and then lifted himself to his feet. He did not feel quite so wobbly. His head was clearer now, too. He stepped off the boat onto the dock, Cailie following. It suddenly struck him—for no reason other than the absence of any other possibility after such a grueling ride—that they must be in Key West.

Cailie guided him past rows of sleeping pelicans awaiting fishermen with the morning catch. They went along a passageway between two boat houses and out to a parking lot where Elizabeth was putting the duffle bags into the back of a Toyota Rav 4.

"Tree, I want you to get into the front passenger seat," Cailie said. She opened the door for him and then guided him inside.

Elizabeth slammed shut the rear hatch door and got behind the wheel. Cailie meantime slipped into the back seat and leaned forward so that the snout of the Glock rested against the base of Tree's neck. "Just letting you know I'm here," Cailie said.

Elizabeth cast what Tree thought was a furtive glance in his direction, but didn't say anything. She started the car forward.

———————

Thunder rumbled ominously as Elizabeth drove swiftly through the empty residential streets of Key West. Lightning lit the roadway for an instant, and then reduced it to a darkness intersected by the Rav 4's headlights.

Elizabeth turned a corner and Tree saw that they were back on Whitehead Street, at the Hemingway Estate. Elizabeth turned onto Olivia Street and pulled over to the curb.

She switched off the motor and took a deep breath, as though steeling herself for what was to come. What, Tree wondered, was to come? Elizabeth threw him another look, as if to say, *I tried to warn you!* But she quickly pulled her eyes away and was out the door. Cailie jabbed the gun barrel against his neck. "All right, Tree. This is where you make your exit."

On the street, Elizabeth opened the rear hatch. Cailie produced a key and called to Elizabeth. "Undo Tree's handcuffs will you?"

Elizabeth looked sharply at Cailie. "Are you sure?"

"Tree knows that if he tries anything, I'll shoot him."

Elizabeth took the key from Cailie and then stepped behind Tree. A moment later, the handcuffs came off, and Cailie moved back a couple of paces to get a better view of her target in case she had to shoot it.

Elizabeth produced a key of her own and went over to a door embedded in the wall running the length of the street. She inserted it into the lock turned it, and the door creaked open. "All set," she called out as she disappeared inside.

"Okay, Tree, pick up those duffle bags and follow her," Cailie said.

That's why he was still alive, he decided. They needed a packhorse. He lifted the bags out of the Rav 4 and then followed Elizabeth through the door.

It was as if he had dropped down the rabbit hole into a darkness broken only by the outlines of palm fronds and dense foliage.

Cailie crowded behind him. "Put the bags down, Tree, and then step away."

He dropped the bags to the ground. Cailie bent to unzip one of them, pulling out two Pelican flashlights and the trenching tool. She handed Elizabeth a flashlight and threw Tree the trenching tool. He should have caught it adroitly, just like they do in the movies. But this wasn't the movies: he dropped it.

"Honestly, Tree, you're such a klutz," Cailie said, rising with her gun in one hand, the Pelican flashlight in the other. Tree bent to pick up the digging tool.

Cailie said, "Now we're going to follow our friend Elizabeth and she's going to show you where to dig."

Tree turned to Elizabeth. "You're kidding. This is where you buried the ten million?"

"I keep telling you, there isn't ten million." Elizabeth sounded irritated.

"Old washed-up spies trying to kick start a second career for themselves, but not having much success until the president of Tajikistan fell into their laps," Tree said. "You collected the money from the president's man, Dr. Edgar Bunya. But then when it became apparent Miram Shah and Zoran were basically phonies, that they couldn't really help Emomali Rahmon get into the country, you and Dearlove decided to keep the money for yourselves and rip off the other two.

"But then Edgar came after you, and you knew you were going to need some muscle." Tree looked at Cailie. "That's where you came in, Cailie. Once you and Elizabeth hooked up, it didn't take long to decide that the easiest way to keep all the money for yourselves was to get rid of the others. You weren't in Key West to follow me—I probably came as quite a shock. You were there to kill Hank Dearlove. I'm still not sure why you saved me from Edgar Bunya, other than the fact that my body lying around Key West would have needlessly complicated things. Edgar was the last hurdle you had to overcome, and maybe the most dangerous. But tonight he's swimming with the fishes."

"You're forgetting about one other impediment," Cailie said.

"What's that?"

"You," she said. "What nobody counted on was Shah bringing you into the mix. So good on you, Tree. You fooled everyone. But it's too late for the clever detective. We don't have the time. So let's get a move on."

Another rumble of thunder was accompanied by a spatter of raindrops as Elizabeth started down a pathway that in the light of the Pelican flash wound through the thick undergrowth. Eventually they broke into a clearing near one of the giant palms scattered throughout the property. Elizabeth stopped, looked around, saw something familiar and pointed to the ground. "There you go, Mr. Callister. That's where you dig."

Tree took a deep breath and went to work.

———

He thrust the point of the blade into the ground, expecting to encounter a sandy undersurface. In fact, the soil he dug into was moist and easily turned. As he worked away by the light of the Pelican flashlights held by Cailie and Elizabeth, he glanced at the women from time to time, his mind swirling, trying to think of a way out of this.

He said to Cailie, "I suppose this is the ultimate revenge, isn't it? Chris spends the rest of his life in jail. You end up rich—and you get to kill me."

He looked at Elizabeth. "But the question is, what are you going to do with Elizabeth here? She's going to become inconvenient as soon as I dig up the money, isn't she?"

He snapped his fingers.

"Wait a minute. That's it. Elizabeth won't be inconvenient if you kill her and make it look as if the two of us got into an argument over the buried money and ended up killing each other. You're not that greedy; you'll even leave something behind to make it look good. No one will ever know about your involvement, no one will be the wiser—and you'll be rich."

Cailie said in a tense voice, "Shut up, Tree."

As Tree resumed his digging, he saw Cailie's eyes flick nervously in Elizabeth's direction. But Elizabeth just grinned and said, "You can hardly blame Mr. Callister for thinking that way. After all, Cailie, you do have the gun."

"Yes, I do," Cailie said. "I do have the gun."

"That gun is very important to you, I know," Elizabeth said.

"Let's finish this," Cailie said.

"But it's not going to mean much," Elizabeth said. "The gun, I mean."

"No?" Cailie said.

"Were you really planning to shoot me?" Elizabeth asked Cailie.

"Of course not," Cailie said. "Why would I do that?"

The words were barely out of her mouth before Joseph Trembath appeared out of the darkness. Tree no sooner recognized him and saw the gun, then Trembath was pulling the trigger.

# 34

Cailie looked vaguely shocked, her head snapping back, the breath screaming out of her. It was the most astonishing thing, Tree thought. One moment she was there, the next moment she was a lifeless heap on the recently-turned ground—a heap somehow still clinging to that Glock pistol.

The shooting signaled the gods to open the heavens and deluge the duplicitous earth.

Through the falling rain, a big lion with a black mane charged him. Tree could not make his legs move. He was Francis Macomber, in a bad place, frozen with fear.

"So sorry, old man"

The lion vanished, and rain-soaked, hard-faced Trembath—no sign of the jovial Englishman tonight—jumped into focus, pointing the gun that was about to end Francis Macomber's cowardice and Tree Callister's life.

Another voice echoed through the rain: "No!"

Elizabeth Traven lurched in front of Tree as Trembath's gun went off.

She cried out. It took Tree a moment to realize she had been shot. Trembath, seeing what he had done, shouted something as Elizabeth's legs went out from under her and she collapsed to her knees near Cailie. She looked around, as if confused by what had just happened.

Tree did not even think about it. He just swung the entrenching tool he held, swinging it with all his might at Trembath's astonished face. The steel edge of the blade sank into Trembath's cheek and then ripped through his nose, sending out a crimson spray.

Trembath staggered back, screaming. His gun went off again, and the lion came back, galloping toward Tree, coming to finish him off.

Tree raised the entrenching tool, using its pointed edge as a spear, thrusting it hard against Trembath's chest.

The point didn't sink in very far, but it was enough to stop the lion's forward motion.

Trembath fell back raising the gun, and Tree was certain he was about to be shot. The sound of the gunshot reverberated through the rain-swept night. Tree waited for the bullet to smack into him.

Except the bullet failed to arrive.

Instead, Trembath dropped his gun and fell to the ground. Now Tree saw Elizabeth sitting up, holding Cailie's Glock.

Tree knelt down to her. Elizabeth allowed the gun to drop from her hand. Her eyes fluttered and she tried on a smile that did not fit very well.

"Here we are, Mr. Callister. What do you think of this?"

"Not a whole lot, Mrs. Traven."

She tried a better smile. "You fooled me again."

"We keep fooling one another. Why did you do that?"

"What did I do?"

"You saved my life."

"Did I? Imagine that."

And then she was gone. Tree held her for a time before he gently lowered her to the ground. He got to his feet, thought about it, and then went over to Cailie's body. He went through the pockets of her jeans without finding his cell phone. She must have tossed it over the side when they were at sea. But he did find a set of keys attached to a plain silver ring. A small metal license plate also hung from the ring. It read, KOPPER1. He shoved the keys into his pocket.

Then he went over to the hole he had dug. The gunshots would soon bring the police. He started digging again.

Something moved at the edge of the clearing. Tree stopped to see what it was. A six-toed ginger cat came into view, its eyes piercing, its tail stiff and twitching. Tree stared at the cat, and the cat stared back at him.

# 35

By the time Tree turned the Rav 4 onto Truman Avenue, the rain had stopped. He got to the turnoff for North Roosevelt Boulevard remembering that would put him on A1A. A1A swept him away from the island onto the interlinked causeways crossing the keys, past Marathon and Big Pine Key and then Key Largo. By now everything was locked up against the dampness of the night, the world plunged into darkness until the lights of Miami International Airport blazed through the post-rain haze.

He turned onto the Florida Turnpike going north to I-75. By five o'clock in the morning, he was speeding through Big Cypress National Preserve, an hour outside Naples. He was surprised he had gotten this far, expecting a fleet of police cars to descend on him in hot pursuit, lights flashing. But then maybe, just maybe, he had done everything close enough to right back at the Hemingway house to get away with this—at least until he finished what he needed to do.

He thought about Cailie who probably believed she would be able to eliminate the competition for the missing ten million dollars, but either she didn't know about, or hadn't counted on, Trembath being hooked up with Elizabeth.

Trembath he could understand. It was his job to eliminate Cailie, correctly divining that if they did not take care of her, she would take care of them. Trembath probably hadn't expected Tree to be part of it, and had little choice but to get rid of him along with Cailie—and make it look as if they had killed one another, not illogical considering their connection to Chris.

What mystified Tree was why Elizabeth stepped in front of the bullet meant for him. Did she care more than he ever imagined? Or was it a spontaneous gesture, an instant of terribly misplaced loyalty to a long-time adversary? Or maybe she had just stumbled at the wrong moment. Whatever it was, it had cost Elizabeth her life—and saved his.

He had briefly considered sticking around to try to explain to the police what had happened, but decided there was no time. Soon enough they would be everywhere and it would be too late to do anything. By now they had discovered the three bodies in the Hemingway compound. Initially, it would look as though Trembath had shot the two women before one of them shot him.

Once they had identified the bodies there would be more questions than answers but if his luck held none of it would lead to him. Even if they were able to connect the dots and arrive at Tree's doorstep, they would not arrive for a while. That would give him enough time, and right now, time was what he needed.

As he reached the outskirts of Fort Myers, daylight streaked a cloudless sky to begin another perfect Florida morning. It was just past seven when he pulled into the parking lot at the marina adjacent to Doc Ford's Restaurant. He went over to where he had parked the Beetle, seemingly an eternity ago, found a chamois cloth in the back and spent the next few minutes rubbing down the interior and exterior of the Rav 4, removing any traces of his presence. Then he locked the Rav 4 and got into the Beetle and started the engine.

At this time of the morning, there was almost no traffic coming off the bridge onto San Carlos Boulevard. The Beetle was just about the only car on the causeway to Sanibel Island. He was dead tired as he pulled into an empty space outside the condominium on Sea Bell Road. It didn't matter. He had to keep going. He opened the glove compartment and reached into the box of latex gloves Todd Jackson had given him. If Tree was going to be a detective and find dead bodies, he should at least be wearing protective gloves, Todd said.

He tried a couple of the keys on Cailie's silver key chain until he found the one that opened the door to her condo. He spent some time struggling into the gloves before stepping into the dim interior. The closed blinds kept out the morning sun. He shut the door behind him and stood listening to the soft hum of the central air conditioning.

At first glance the apartment, with its flat white walls unadorned with pictures, was as anonymous as the woman who rented it. Slowly, however, as Tree's eyes became accustomed to the dimness, he began to pick out certain things: the laptop on the desk by the windows; the files piled beside the computer. More papers on the counter forming a barrier between the galley kitchen and the living room.

Something moved through the darkness, causing Tree to gasp. Then he saw that it was a black and white cat. Everywhere he went, cats, he thought. The cat leapt onto the computer desk, turning its fine, feline head to regard Tree, cat's eyes gleaming out of the darkness.

Tree went over and carefully reached out to scratch its ears. The animal didn't seem to mind at all. It closed its eyes with pleasure and began to purr.

The cat trailed Tree into the bedroom. Cailie hadn't made the double bed the previous morning. Gym clothes were discarded on the carpet. Casual, stylish clothing hung neatly in the closets facing the bed. Women's cosmetics and lotions crowded the bathroom counter. She had left a bath towel on the floor. He opened one of the drawers below the counter. Inside was a .38 police revolver—Cailie never far from a gun. He left it where it was and closed the drawer.

He went back to the living room and sat at the laptop. The cat leapt onto the desk and settled nearby, rubbing the side of its head against the edge of the computer screen. Cailie said that she had a confession linking Chris to the murder of his wife that she had recorded. She would have turned the recording over to the police, but he was willing to bet she had kept a copy for herself. He did not want to know, but at the same time he had to. He had to understand for himself what his son had said, and finally know for certain his guilt or innocence.

As he expected, access to the laptop was password encrypted. He thought of something and got Cailie's set of keys out of his pocket. Attached to the chain was a miniature metal license plate, Kopper1, stamped into its surface.

He typed Kopper1 into the password box, hit return, and—

That wasn't the password.

Then a sound—someone attempting to insert a key into the lock of the front door. Tree froze, fingers poised over the keyboard.

Whoever was at the door tried again, and this time succeeded. Tree heard the door open and then close. The cat jumped down from the desk and padded across the carpet. Tree had just time enough to duck beneath the desk before he heard footsteps coming uncertainly toward him.

From his vantage point, he could see a man's legs move into view. The cat appeared, rubbing against the intruder's legs a moment before he fell heavily against a wall, swearing. Then he called out, "Cailie? Are you here? Cailie?"

The slurred voice of Sanibel Detective Owen Markfield.

Tree tensed beneath the desk. All Markfield had to do was turn on a light, and that would be it.

But Markfield didn't turn on any lights. Instead, he straightened himself, and Tree could make out a cell phone being pulled from the pocket of his jeans with some difficulty. Sharp little electronic alerts filled the room—Markfield poking out a number. The ensuing silence was broken by Markfield's labored breathing. Finally, he said, "It's me. I'm in your apartment. The cat is here, incidentally. Vienna? Is that its name? Vienna and me, we're waiting. Where are you?"

He would learn the answer soon enough, Tree mused. But he would never hear it from Cailie Fisk.

Markfield dropped the cell phone a few feet from where Tree crouched against the desk. He bent to pick it up. He only had to glance over, and he would see Tree. But as he bent forward, the cat swished against him, and the detective nearly lost his balance. He swore again, kicking at the cat

"Get out of here!" he yelled, before lurching over to an armchair. Tree heard him fall heavily into it. He groaned loudly, followed by more silence. Tree remained in place, hardly daring to breathe. He peered around the desk, straining to see where Markfield was.

A loud, honking made Tree jump. He rose from behind the desk for a view of Markfield through the dimness, slumped in the chair, head thrown back, mouth hanging open, Sanibel's most officious representative of law and order at drunken rest, snoring loudly.

Tree slowly let out his breath, before turning back to the laptop. He leaned over the keyboard and typed VIENNA.

A moment later, he was on Cailie's home screen. A photograph of Kendra Dean smiled at him, luminous, caught in sunlight, the way Cailie undoubtedly preferred to remember her.

An audio file was on the desk top. He stared at the screen. Kendra smiled back from the grave, daring him to play that file.

He shut down the computer and closed the screen before disconnecting the power cord. He picked up the laptop and started out of the apartment. Vienna had returned to her perch atop the desk, taking silent note of Tree's departure.

# 36

The sun was already hot, and the humidity had crept across the beautifully manicured lawn running up to the Dayton house, making it hard for Tree to breathe as he approached the front door.

Or maybe it wasn't the humidity.

He rang the doorbell twice before Vera Dayton answered. She wore a white caftan, her hair pulled back from a surprised face without makeup.

"Tree," she said. She touched the edges of her jaw, as if aware she wasn't wearing her mask this morning.

"I need to talk to you," Tree said.

She stood there, her mouth opening, nothing coming out.

"Can I come in?"

She rallied enough to say, "Is Fredericka with you?"

"No, I wanted to talk to you alone."

She nodded and stepped back to allow him entry. She led him along a hallway into a brilliant living room as white as an elephant's graveyard.

"I'm sorry," she said, fighting to maintain her composure, "I wasn't expecting company." As if she would have been different if she was. "Please, sit down."

He settled on white easy chair while she occupied a white sofa facing him.

"Do you mind if I smoke?" she said.

"No, of course not."

She reached into a silver box on the glass-topped end table beside the sofa. It was a type he hadn't seen since he watched his parents smoking in the 1950s. She withdrew a cigarette and then lifted up the silver lighter beside the silver box. He got to his feet, took the lighter from her, flicked the wheel, and was rewarded with a tongue of blue flame. He held the flame to her cigarette until it was successfully lit. He could not remember the last time he had lighted anyone's cigarette—or how long it had been since he saw someone send gray puffs of smoke into the air.

"I hadn't smoked for years, but after Ray's death and all this confusion about the business..." She allowed her voice to trail off.

"Yes, after Ray's death I imagine things can't have been easy," Tree said.

She took another puff and said, "Why are you here, Tree?"

"It's about Ray," Tree said.

"He never liked you, you know."

"Well, I don't think we liked each other. I don't think you liked him, either, Vera."

She gave him a hard look through a veil of smoke. "How could you say that?"

"Because it helps explain why you murdered him."

She stared at him. The hard look softened. The cigarette did not move. Gray smoke curled into the air. "That's ridiculous," she said in a small voice.

"When you found out Ray was having an affair with my son's wife, you went down to the house in Naples, and you shot him and then made it look like suicide—or did your best to make it look that way, which given the state of Ray's life at the time, wasn't hard to do."

Her face had gone as white as the room. "This is preposterous," she said.

"That's why you came to see me at the office. You were worried that if the police thought Chris killed Kendra, it might refocus attention on Ray. If he didn't kill her, then why would he commit suicide?"

"That's not true," she said.

"What I can't figure out, Vera, is why you told Cailie Dean. It doesn't make any sense."

"I didn't tell her anything," she said, not very convincingly.

"Vera, I've got Cailie's laptop."

"How do you have that?" Vera sounded surprised—and alarmed.

"Never mind how, but I have it. On the way over here, I listened to Cailie's conversation with you that she secretly recorded. She lied to me. She suggested she had recorded a conversation with Chris, but it's with you."

"I want you to get out of here, Tree. I want you to leave this house."

"If I walk out, I go to the police."

"And if you don't?"

"Then we talk this out. Ray is dead. So is Cailie."

She looked at him in surprise. "Cailie is dead?"

Tree nodded. "You'll hear more about it later. It doesn't matter how I know, but I do. What's done is done. Right now, I'm only interested in protecting my son and making sure he doesn't spend the rest of his life in jail."

Vera rose to fetch a cut-glass ashtray and spent some time mashing the half-smoked cigarette into it.

"That's what brought Callie to me in the first place," Vera said. She carried the ashtray back to the sofa. "She had questions about her sister's murder, and she wasn't satisfied with the answers she was getting."

Reseated, Vera placed the ashtray on the sofa beside her and then leaned forward with her elbows on her knees. "She didn't believe Ray murdered Kendra. I told her he didn't do it."

Tree felt his stomach twist into a knot. "Except that we know he did."

"Before he died, Ray swore to me he didn't kill her."

"I know. That's what you told Cailie. That's what made her start to think that maybe Ray wasn't the killer and Chris was."

"He didn't want me to shoot him." Vera said this in a way that suggested the idea of shooting husbands wasn't so unusual.

"But it didn't work," Tree said.

She reached over to the silver box for another cigarette. "I hated Ray, hated what he did to our marriage, the way he betrayed me."

"Ray would have said anything at that point," Tree said. "Told any lie in order to save his life."

Vera held the cigarette between her fingers. "But what he said was, he didn't kill Kendra."

This time Vera lit the cigarette herself. She drew deeply on it and then raised her head to let more smoke into the air. By now the room had filled with a pungent tobacco smell.

"That wouldn't have been enough to go to the police with," Tree said. "But it was enough to convince Cailie that she could lie, say that Chris confessed to her, and if you had a detective who was infatuated, and an assistant district attorney out for blood, it might be enough to get Chris indicted for his wife's murder. Not a great case, maybe, but a case."

"You're supposing Cailie was lying," Vera said.

"She was lying," Tree said with a lot more conviction than he was feeling.

Vera said, "So we both have a dirty little secret, Tree. You don't want the world to know your son killed his wife. I would prefer that everyone continued to think Ray committed suicide."

"What makes you so certain I wouldn't turn my son in if I knew he had killed his wife?"

"You won't allow yourself to believe that. If you accuse me of killing my husband, however, then the rest of it will come out. Neither of us wants that, so we keep each other's secrets."

Tree rose to his feet. Vera said, "Aren't you forgetting something?"

"What's that, Vera?"

"The recording Cailie made."

Tree looked at her. "What are you going to do about the Dayton supermarkets?"

She flicked ash into the ashtray.

"Are you going to sell them to Freddie and her group?"

"Will that make it easier for me to get hold of that recording?"

"I have Cailie's laptop," Tree said.

"Where is it?"

"It's in the car."

"And that's the only copy?"

Tree nodded. "I don't imagine she would have given it to the police. Otherwise, you would have heard from them by now."

Vera reached for another cigarette before she said, "Why don't you go out to your car and get it?"

# 37

The Key West police found the bodies of Elizabeth Traven, Cailie Dean, and Joseph Trembath, as well as the five hundred thousand dollars in cash it appeared they had just dug up with a Glock entrenching tool on the grounds of the Hemingway Estate before a fight broke out, and they all ended up dead.

The assistant district attorney said he had little choice but to drop the murder charges against Chris Callister, since the prosecution's main witness was dead. The ADA intimated he was not convinced of Chris's innocence. There was, as Tree suspected, no talk of any recorded confession.

Chris decided to go back to Chicago. Sanibel Island was too small and too much had happened to him here. Sticking around, he said, would only encourage the police to find something else with which to charge him. Chicago would give him some distance from an unfriendly island and allow him to start over. There were no ghosts in Chicago—or at least not so many.

Tree drove Chris out to the Fort Myers International Airport. Chris wanted his dad to drop him off at the curb, but Chris was wrestling with three bags so Tree insisted on parking the car and accompanying his son into the airport, carrying one of the bags.

At two o'clock in the afternoon the main concourse was all but empty. Tree stood awkwardly with Chris outside the security area. Every time he looked at him, Tree tried hard not to see a killer looking back.

Sometimes he succeeded.

"Would you tell Freddie I'm really happy for her," Chris said. "If anyone can run a chain of supermarkets down here, it's Freddie."

"I'll tell her that," Tree said.

"It's going to be a big change in your life, I guess."

"I'm not sure," Tree said. "The deal is supposed to go through in the next week or so. We'll see."

"Look, Dad," Chris said, "I know I haven't said much, and I know I haven't always sounded as though I do, but I really appreciate everything you've done for me."

"I'm not sure how much I've done," Tree said. Knowing that was nowhere near the truth.

"If it wasn't for you, if you didn't believe in me, I'd still be sitting in a jail cell."

Did he believe in his son? Yes, yes, he did, he silently insisted. He told himself that over and over again. Chris was innocent. Cailie was deceitful and untrustworthy. Ray Dayton had been fighting for his life when he swore to his wife he didn't murder Kendra.

As if he had been reading Tree's mind, Chris embraced his father with tears in his eyes. Tree could hardly believe it; a son being emotional about his father.

"Call me," Tree said. "Let me know how you're doing."

"I will." Chris quickly wiped the tears away and grabbed at his luggage. Then he paused and Tree was struck with the wild notion Chris was about to confess. The moment passed. Chris cast one more glance at Tree and then hurried away.

Tree watched until Chris had made his way through the security gauntlet, feeling at once relieved and sad, uncertain if he had regained a son or lost him for good.

Choking back surprising tears, he started across the concourse, almost running into Owen Markfield.

"I thought I'd come to witness the touching father-son farewell for myself," Markfield said.

Tree didn't say anything.

"I still think he murdered his wife."

Tree remained silent. "What's more," Markfield continued, "I think you lied and cheated and you may have even murdered in order to cover up for him."

"It's always good to see you, Detective," Tree said.

He went to go past, but Markfield blocked his path. "Also there is the matter of the missing nine million, five hundred thousand dollars."

"I don't know what you're talking about."

"The government of Tajikistan is making a lot of noise about an American cabal led by Henry Dearlove that ripped it off to the tune of ten million dollars for services that were never rendered. The Key West police have been working with the FBI and the State Department on the investigation. The thinking is that your friend Elizabeth Traven was in cahoots with Cailie Fisk or Cailie Dean, and they conspired with Joseph Trembath to kill off Dearlove and other members of the cabal and keep the money themselves. They were in the process of digging up the loot when some sort of falling out occurred that ended with the three of them dead. About five hundred thousand dollars was recovered at the scene. The question is, where is the rest of the money?"

"Maybe you shouldn't be too quick to believe the government of Taji—whatever it's called," Tree said.

"The Key West police suspect there was a fourth person at the scene," Markfield continued. "The Fort Myers Beach police have found a car registered to Joseph Trembath parked in a lot at a marina over there. The speculation is that a fourth man got away from the Hemingway house with the money, drove back to Fort Myers and dumped the car."

"This is all very interesting," Tree said. "But I don't know what it's got to do with me."

"Cailie Dean, of course, turned out to be the sister of your son's murdered wife. She went undercover using an assumed name to get close to Chris. She extracted a confession from him, and was to be our main witness.

"You've been mixed up with Elizabeth Traven in the past. Incidentally, I forgot to mention the yacht leased by Elizabeth that was found moored dockside at Key West."

"I didn't even know Elizabeth was interested in yachts," Tree said.

"Also, Joseph Trembath was working for Miram Shah who was a client of yours, was he not?"

"That's right," Tree said. "I knew Elizabeth obviously, and my son, not knowing who she was, got mixed up with Cailie, but I don't believe he confessed anything to her."

"I think you are that fourth man, Callister. You were involved with all of them. You killed Cailie because she had evidence against your son. You murdered the other two to cover up Cailie's murder and then you took the missing money for yourself."

"Sure, it's in the trunk of my car," Tree said. "Do you want me to get it for you?"

"Where were you the night all this went down?"

"I wasn't in Key West, that's for sure."

"Then where were you, Callister? Your wife was in New York so she can't provide you with an alibi,"

"I'll tell you what, Detective. Why don't you phone Edith Goldman? She's my lawyer. If you want to formally question me, let's do it with her present."

"Maybe I will do just that. You are going down for this, I swear you are."

"This is all a lot of crap, Markfield, and you know it. I would have to be a whole lot smarter than I am to pull off what you're describing."

"I think you specialize in making people believe you're less than what you are, Callister. I've seen you pull that stunt before. It works for others, maybe, but it doesn't work for me."

"No, I'm pretty much as dumb as I look. Now will you get out of the way?"

"This isn't over. I'm going to spend the time it takes to get that money back and nail your ass."

Markfield brushed past and walked off down the concourse.

# 38

The thirty-two-foot Cobalt, in all its gleaming black and white glory, was the replacement for Rex's destroyed *Former Actor*. Ivory-colored seating swept elegantly away from a control panel that would have looked at home inside a space craft. The boat already had been christened *Former Actor Too*.

Tree along with Freddie and Todd Jackson and many island Chamber of Commerce members had contributed to a boat fund for Rex. A local marina happened to be sitting on the repossessed Cobalt and was willing to let it go at a fire sale price.

Now everyone gathered on the dock at Port Sanibel Marina to admire the new craft as crimson light fell along its shiny surfaces. At this time of the afternoon *Former Actor Too* appeared to float on a dream.

"It just goes to show you," Rex said with as much excitement in his voice as Rex could muster about anything, "sometimes it's not so bad when someone blows up your boat."

"Yeah, you end up with a better one," Todd Jackson said.

Rex turned to Tree. "Why do I suspect you're behind this?"

"Not me, it was all I could do to blow up the first boat," Tree said.

Rex, in a burst of affection Tree seldom saw from his old friend, hugged him. "We've been friends too damn long, that's the problem," Rex said in a choked voice. 'We're starting to be nice to one another."

"Yeah we've got to watch that," Tree said, unexpectedly moved.

Everyone crowded aboard the *Former Actor Too*. Rex broke out champagne and they all toasted Rex's new boat, and, if truth be told, the happy fact of Rex in their lives. Rex again told the story of how he battled flames and high waves to reach the safety of Useppa Island after the *Former Actor* sank beneath the waves.

"At the end of it, there's a great story to tell, that's the important thing," Rex said later when he and Tree had a moment alone. "But what I still don't get is exactly *who* blew up my boat."

"The police think it was Dr. Edgar Bunya, the guy you saw at the Visitors Center, although they have yet to find his body."

"So he killed the guy on Useppa Island?"

Tree shook his head. "That was probably Cailie Fisk. Edgar got there with his goons looking for Elizabeth, found the body, and decided they didn't want to stick around trying to explain things to the police. We showed up as they were trying to make their escape."

"So they let us have it with a grenade. Kind of an over-reaction, don't you think?"

"Well, that was Dr. Bunya for you." Tree said. "He probably saw me, worried that I recognized him and could place him at the scene of a crime, and decided to do something about it."

"Then it's all your fault," Rex said.

"It usually is," Tree said.

"That's what I've been trying to tell you for the past forty years."

Later, Rex told everyone about Jack Palance when he was making *I Died A Thousand Times* and the funny way Jack had of peeling a banana.

As she listened, Freddie took Tree's hand, tacit acknowledgment perhaps of how close she had come lately to losing this flawed husband of hers. He marveled for the millionth time at how fortunate he was to have this beautiful woman in a life that on this sun-drenched Florida evening was not so bad after all.

He was alive, and his son was not going to jail for the rest of his life. He'd had to do things he never imagined doing, and along the way sign a deal or two with the devil—or so it seemed. But at the end, the good guys lived to fight another day and the bad guys were mostly gone. Except he could not decide which of those categories he fell into. When you are trying to survive the charging lions, sometimes the line between good and bad got blurred. Francis Macomber would have understood that.

"Tree?" Freddie said as they turned onto the causeway headed back to Sanibel.

That brought him out of his reverie. "Yes?"

"You were far, far away."

"I was in Africa, facing the lion."

"What lion?"

"The one in the Hemingway short story," he said.

"Oh, Lord," Freddie groaned. "That's such a lousy story. Macomber's wife is awful. Imagine breaking down in tears just because your husband is smart enough to run away from a charging lion."

"She sleeps with the white hunter because her husband is a coward."

"That's so incredibly dumb."

"I read that story as a kid. All my life I've wondered, if the lion charged, would I stand my ground or would I turn and run?"

"So after all these years what have you decided, Tree?"

"What do you mean?"

"Would you stand your ground or would you run?"

"I always thought I would run," Tree said.

She smiled and said, "Smart man."

"But I didn't. To my absolute surprise, I didn't run."

They rode in silence onto the second span of the causeway. "Why do I think you're not telling me everything," Freddie said, finally. "Why do I think that somehow you were mixed up in that business in Key West."

"What makes you think that?" Tree said.

"Because Elizabeth Traven was there, and my experience with you is that when she is in trouble, you're not far away."

"This time I wasn't much help to her," Tree said.

"You couldn't find her," Freddie said.

Tree hesitated before he said, "That's right, I couldn't find her. I looked hard enough, but in the end, I couldn't find her. I'm not much of a detective, I'm afraid."

Freddie gently took his hand and squeezed it and said quietly, "Tree, I don't want my husband facing lions. I want my husband to run away from them because I love him and I want him *alive*."

"And I didn't have an affair with Cailie Fisk."

"Cailie Dean," Freddie said.

"I didn't have an affair with her, either."

"I never thought you did."

"I love you," he said.

"I know you do."

"If I have you, I can confront anything. Even the lions."

"We will take on the lions together," Freddie said.

Tree said, "They think I'm holding on to nine and a half million dollars that doesn't belong to me."

Freddie stole a quick glance as she drove. "You're kidding, aren't you?"

"I know you don't like it when I keep things from you."

"Who thinks you have nine million dollars?"

"Among other people, the police."

"But you don't have it. Do you?"

Tree didn't say anything.

"Tree," she said insistently, "reassure me that you are as honest as the day you were born—or at least as honest as the day I married you. Tell me you don't have that money."

Tree remained silent.

"Tree, say something."

On San Carlos Bay pelicans swooped over pleasure craft leaving silvery wakes in the dying light of the day.

"Tree?"

# Acknowledgments

Writing a third Tree Callister adventure was a joy thanks to the great team that sees me through every time I set out to do one of these books.

My wife Kathy Lenhoff not only makes life an endless wonder, she also serves as first reader and first line of defense when it comes to spotting her husband's errors. Thank you, darling, for your love—and your willingness to keep reading draft after draft.

My son Joel Ruddy read an early draft and, as always, his enthusiasm keeps my spirits up and makes me believe I might be onto something. Erin Ruddy is not only the world's greatest daughter, but working with her on the novel she is writing, made me confront the shortcomings in my own book.

I am blessed with a team of first rate editors who constantly pull me back from the cliff edge. David Kendall meticulously went through the manuscript, holding my feet to the fire all the way; Bob Burt, as tough as an old boot when it comes to editing, uncovered plot inconsistencies and asked questions that forced me to dig deeper into the story and make it better.

Finally, Ray Bennett, formerly of the *Hollywood Reporter*, and now editor of London, England's *Cue Entertainment* magazine, brought nearly fifty years of editorial experience to the final line edit of the book. Nothing is more comforting than knowing, after all these years of friendship, you've still got my back, Raymundo.

It's becoming a November tradition for my neighbor Kim Hunter and I to drive to Florida to launch a new novel. We travel in his pickup truck as befits a bestselling author like myself. Kim is a great driver, but he resists my suggestion that he wear a chauffeur's cap and hold the door open for me when I get out of the truck.

Bridgit Stone-Budd has done so much to give *The Sanibel Sunset Detective* adventures a distinctive appearance with her highly original covers. You've succeeded again, Bridgit, and your patience and professionalism with an author who doesn't always know what he wants, is much appreciated. And speaking of patience, I have to mention Brian Frommer, the talented designer who does the posters for the Tree Callister novels. Despite the fact that I must drive him crazy, Brian always produces outstanding work.

My brother Ric has become such an integral part of the publishing process that I seriously understate the case when I say none of this would be possible without him. Not only did he provide the original idea for these books, but he oversees the printing process. He is a constant source of support and encouragement, and if that isn't enough, he also served as technical advisor for all things nautical in the book. My sister-in-law Alicia, with endless good humor, puts up with me underfoot for weeks on end—and if she likes a Tree Callister novel, I know I've done something right.

Finally, as I finish this latest volume, I think of Brian Vallée, the publisher of West-End Books who was unstinting in his support of these novels, and who exited far too early. Thanks yet again old pal; you continue to be missed every day.

And I can't thank Brian without also thanking his partner, Nancy Rahtz, who allows the West-End Book imprint to continue, headed for bigger and better things.

# Don't Miss The Previous
# Tree Callister Novels

## The Sanibel Sunset Detective

Everyone on Sanibel Island, Florida thinks former newspaperman Tree Callister is crazy to become a private detective. The only client he can attract is a twelve-year-old boy who has seven dollars with which to hire Tree to find his mother.

## The Sanibel Sunset Detective  Returns

The beautiful wife of a disgraced media mogul is certain her husband is having an affair. She hires Tree Callister to get the evidence. Then the mogul turns up dead on Sanibel Island, and not only is Tree's client arrested, but he finds himself accused of being an accessory to murder.

## Coming Soon

## The Two Sanibel Sunset Detectives

ronbase@ronbase.com
ronbase.wordpress.com
ronbase.com

CPSIA information can be obtained
at www.ICGtesting.com
Printed in the USA
FFOW03n1748210117
31546FF

9 780973 695564